The Wrong Husband 2

B.M. Hardin

Copyright©2016
David Weaver Presents(kindle)
Savvily Published LLC(Paperback Edition)
ISBN-13:
978-0692670255
ISBN-10:
0692670254

Dedication

This book is dedicated to a few special superstar readers, Farrah Clark, Karitha James, Nicole Coleman, Mariah Gray, Brenda Lang, Bettzy Crosby, and Michelle Williams.

Thank you all for your support and for following me on my writing journey. It is truly a blessing to have supporters like you in my corner. Thank you!

Acknowledgements

First and foremost, I want to thank my Heavenly Father for my talents and my gifts and each and every story that he has placed in me.

It is an honor and a privilege to be living my dream and walking in my purpose and for that I am forever thankful.

Also to all of my family, friends, critiques, supporters, readers and everyone else, thank you for believing in me and allowing me to share my gifts with you.

Your support truly means the world to me!

B.M. Hardin

Author B.M. Hardin's contact info:

Facebook: http://www.facbook.com/authorbm

Twitter: @BMHardin1

Instagram: @bm_hardin

Email:bmhardinbooks@gmail.com

The Wrong Husband 2

<u>Prologue:</u>

This is a Recap of The Wrong Husband Part One:

"Why Polo Sassi?"

I took a deep breath.

"He was there. He was easy access. He told me his feelings for me and I allowed them to actually mean something to me because I wasn't happy. Even though I wanted to be happy, I wasn't."

Eddie didn't say anything.

"I never meant to ruin your friendship with Polo or our marriage. I allowed things to go too. I could have stopped them but I didn't."

"Both of you are at fault. But you know what, I forgive you and Polo. Polo and I can never go back to being how we were and you and I may never have what we had, but I forgive you. I have to forgive you for me. I'm tired of being angry Sassi. I talked to your mother and she made me realize that holding on the hurt only continues to hurt the person feeling the pain, while the people that hurt you are moving on with their lives."

"But I'm not moving on Eddie. It took me losing you to realize that I lost the best part of me."

"I just don't believe that Sassi."

"But it's true. You have to still love me Eddie."

"I'll always love you Sassi, but that's just not enough."

We both stopped talking and just sat there.

I tried to think of something that I could say that might have a big impact on him or pull at his heart strings.

Then I thought of something.

"We both did things. You lied to me. I lied and betrayed you. But remember what we said when we took our vows? We'd said until death do us part, and you told me that no matter what I did and no matter what happened, that the only way that you would leave me was if you "woke up dead". You said that you would literally have to die in your sleep because any other way, you would have found a way to live, you would have found a way to keep breathing, just for me. Remember?"

Eddie looked down at the floor.

"Now we're sitting here divorced and I don't want to be. I still love you, and I know that I messed up big time but I need for you to keep your promise to me. I need to you to keep your vow even though I broke a part of mine."

Eddie was speechless.

I could tell that he had a million things going on in his head.

"The second time around is always better. It's always sweeter they say. Things will be different and better, I just know that they will."

I had to get Eddie back.

And I was going to do it.

One day.

One memory.

One word at a time.

"You wouldn't dare."

"Oh, but I would."

Polo threatened to tell Eddie that we'd just had sex again

I'd talked Eddie into going out to dinner with me.

Well, I'd talked him into taking me out to eat since he was the one with the job.

Polo must have a tracking device or something on one of us because out of nowhere, he popped up.

He texted me and told me to meet him near the bathroom.

"We are just having a meal."

"Looks like y'all are trying to work things out to me, but just the other day I had your legs up in the air and you were screaming my name."

Oh how I wanted to tell him that I faked it.

But I knew that would piss him off and he would surely tell Eddie.

"He won't believe you."

Polo laughed.

He walked off and headed for Eddie and I followed him.

"Bro, long time no see," Polo said.

Eddie cringed.

"I'm not your bro Polo. My brother wouldn't have done what you did with my wife."

"Are we still on that? I thought we got past that."

"What is it Polo?"

"I just wanted to come over and see how you have been. I saw Sassi the other day, but I forgot to ask about you."

Eddie looked at me.

"What day was that Sassi? The day that you had on that red shirt and those killer white pants?"

Of course Eddie had seen me that day, so he knew that Polo had seen me too.

Polo opened his mouth and just as he did, in a panic, I picked up the wine bottle off of the table and hit him with it.

Polo fell to the floor, knocked out cold.

Everyone gasped.

"What the hell is wrong with you Sassi? Why did you do that?" Eddie jumped.

"I'm tired of him bothering us Eddie. He just needs to leave me alone. Leave us alone."

Really I'd hit him to keep him from telling him that we'd had sex.

It was the only thing that I knew to do.

The restaurant staff rushed over but Eddie told him that he had everything under control.

He said that Polo was a friend of ours and that it had been an accident.

He explained that I had a disorder and I'd thought that Polo was trying to attack me while having one of my spells.

Eddie shook Polo.'

Polo opened his eyes.

"Eddie?"

"Yeah man, let's get you out of here. See, he knows me," Eddie said to them and he helped Polo up and headed for the door.

I followed behind them, still holding the bottle.

"I'll drive him home, you follow behind us in my car."

I wished that the blow to the head had killed him.

But that would have been too easy and my life just wasn't set up that way.

We pulled up at Polo's house and by then Eddie had told Polo that some girl that he probably used to sleep with came out of nowhere and hit him in the back of the head with a bottle.

Polo was still shaken up and with the knot growing on his head, Eddie suggested the hospital, but Polo refused.

He glanced at me in the car, but Polo didn't say anything.

Eddie helped him into the house and after some time, he came back out.

I got out and headed to the passenger side.

"Sassi, that was crazy!"

"Ever since whatever he has been giving me such a hard time. Harassing me. Popping up. Calling me all the time. I told him over and over again that it was a mistake and I just want him to go away."

"You caused all of this. We all were fine. We had good friendships, we were married. But you chose to sleep with Polo."

"I know. Can you fix it for me? It was a horrible mistake, can you fix it Eddie?"

"What?"

"What is it that you know on Polo? Who did he kill Eddie?"

"What? What are you talking about Sassi?"

"Polo recorded a conversation between you and him. You told him that you thought that I was cheating. You said that if you found out that I was that you were going to kill me. And then you asked Polo could he do it for you…like he did before. Who did he kill Eddie?"

Eddie looked as though he couldn't believe the words coming out of my mouth.

"Never repeat that again Sassi. Ever."

"What did he do before Eddie? To who?"

"Sassi, just let it go. There's no point in going digging around in past things that you have nothing to do with. I'll make sure that Polo leaves you alone from here on out okay? Just don't ever mention that again."

Eddie drove like a bat out of hell down the street.

I turned to look out the window and smiled.

Honestly, I didn't care what it was; if Eddie could get Polo to leave me alone completely, then screw the little secret that they had.

I was just fine with that.

~***~

"I finished it," I squealed in Micki's ear.

My book was finish and I didn't know what to do with myself.

"I'm so proud of you."

"Thank you."

"Now what, do you reach out to the company from the Patrice's will?"

"Yeah. I guess that's the next step. Speaking of, found someone to start dating yet?"

"Actually, I did. He's a white guy. We had our first date the other day. He wants kids and a wife, so I'm hoping that we hit it off. And you?"

"Girl, I'm gonna need more than a few weeks to break Eddie down. But we did have sex again the other day. We were both just horny I guess. But he's still not bending all that much."

"It'll work out."

"I hope so. But someone's ringing the doorbell so I will call you back."

I got up off of the toilet, got myself together and ran down the stairs.

I opened it.

"Eddie, why didn't you just use you key?"

He looked at me as though I'd asked a stupid question.

"I couldn't get to it obviously."

He was carrying both of the boys.

They were both asleep.

He carried them in, laid them on the couch and started to undress them.

"Sassi, what if I came to stay here? Like a roommate or something. I'm always here. I'll sleep down here on the couch. My folks are driving me crazy. I'll start looking for a place as soon as possible. I won't be here longer than a month."

"Yes."

With him under the same roof as me and the kids, I was going to work some magic.

I was going to make Eddie never want to leave.

I was going to get my husband back.

And twenty million dollars too.

Eddie carried the oldest upstairs first.

Once he came back down, I made a suggestion.

"You know you miss us. Let's just work it out Eddie."

"I don't know Sassi. I just don't know."

He picked up our smallest child and then he carried him upstairs too.

In my thoughts, I thought about how many ways I could seduce him and how many ways I could tempt him and make him remember why he loved me and wanted to marry me in the first place.

Wrong husband originally or not, he was all I ever needed.

And I had twenty million reasons that would cosign to that.

A knock at the door stole my attention.

I figured it was Mama since she was supposed to stop by but I was wrong.

It was Polo.

I frowned but he smiled.

He walked right in my house without an invite.

"Excuse me?"

"Eddie told me to meet him here."

What?

"Eddie!" I screamed.

"Why?"

"I don't know Sassi."

"I would appreciate it if you didn't tell him about…"

Polo nodded behind me to Eddie standing on the steps.

He walked down the few that he had left to go, slowly.

He walked directly in front of me.

He held up his hand.

Damn it!

I had been taking a pregnancy test while on the phone with Micki and had left it on the sink.

I totally forgot about it.

I hadn't had a period in a while and figured that it was time to test.

"You're pregnant Sassi. Is it mine? Or is it Polo's?"

I looked back and forth between both of them.

Though originally I was trying to put the baby on Eddie, no matter what, at that moment, and looking at the positive pregnancy test, I had another plan.

Eddie looked at the test, and Polo looked at me.

I took a deep breath.

"It's not mine."

Of course it was mine, but they didn't have to know that.

"What?"

"It's Micki's. She was here earlier and she took a pregnancy test. We started talking while we were waiting for the results and forgot all about it," I lied.

Eddie looked at me.

Polo was staring at me too as though he was trying to decide whether he believe me or not.

"Look, I'll prove it."

I grabbed my phone to call Micki.

She knew I was taking a test and she would lie for me and fall in line with the story with little to no details.

That's what friends were for.

The phone ranged and I looked as the sound of her phone ringing came through the front door.

Micki.

"I was just calling you. Tell them that the pregnancy test it yours," I said to her.

She didn't say anything.

She walked over and stood beside Polo.

All three of them seemed very strange at that moment and I felt uneasy.

Suddenly, Eddie spoke.

"She knows."

"Knows what?" Polo asked.

"Vanessa."

Micki and Polo gasped.

What?

Who and the hell is Vanessa?

I didn't know a Vanessa and I didn't have a clue as to what they were talking about.

"How?" I was surprised to hear Micki ask.

"She said she watched a recording of a conversation that Polo and I had."

Polo looked at Eddie and then at me.

"Damn, you're nosey."

"What the hell is going on? What are y'all talking about? Who is Vanessa?"

I turned to face Eddie.

Micki walked over and stood beside him and out of nowhere, Polo grabbed me from behind.

What?

He somewhat placed me in a choke hold.

It wasn't too tight where he was choking me but it was tight enough where I couldn't get out of it.

"Get the hell off of me Polo! Eddie? Micki? Get him off of me!"

But they both just stood there.

What the hell is happening right now?

I squirmed for a few minutes more and then Polo took his free hand and it was though he was searching for something on my neck.

He found the spot, and pressed firmly on some kind of pressure point, that I didn't even know that I had.

I felt woozy all of a sudden and my eyes became heavy as Polo continued to hold me and press down.

I was passing out.

Or I guess Polo was causing me to pass out in some way.

My body became limp and I could no longer try to get away from Polo.

Closing my eyes, Eddie and Micki started to talk and then suddenly, I didn't see them.

I didn't hear them.

Everything was quiet.

Everything was dark.

Uh oh.

Chapter 1

"Sassi? Sassi? Wake up."

I opened my eyes.

Eddie was standing right in front of me. Immediately my memory kicked in and I started to panic. Without hesitating, I started to throw punches in Eddie's direction. I could hear Eddie screaming but I continued to punch and kick at him.

"Stop it Sassi!"

I ignored him. I felt as though I was in a fight for my life and I'd be damn and I didn't try to fight my way out of here. At least, that's what I'd wanted to believe, but unfortunately my body started to give out on me. After a while, my punches and kicks came to a halt, and I struggled to try to catch my breath. Eddie was still screaming at me, but I searched for something, anything that I could use as a weapon.

"Sassi, what the hell is wrong with you?" Eddie said rubbing his arm and the side of his head.

"Get the hell away from me Eddie!" I managed to scream.

I looked around for Micki and Polo, but they weren't there.

"Where in the hell---,"

Before I could finish my sentence, Eddie started to chuckle.

"You must have had one hell of a bad dream," Eddie shook his head and sat down across from me.

What?

No.

Hell no!

He was lying! I hadn't been dreaming. I was sure of it.

"Dream?"

"Yes. You must've had a bad dream."

I eyed Eddie suspiciously, but he didn't break a sweat.

He just stared at me.

"No. I wasn't dreaming. Stop lying Eddie! That's a load of bull and you know it! I wasn't dreaming! Where is---,"

Without finishing my sentence, I stood up and after taking about two steps, I started to run as though Eddie was chasing me.

I ran up the stairs and headed for my bathroom. I looked on the edge of the sink for the pregnancy test.

Wait...no.

It wouldn't be there because Eddie had come down the stairs with it in his hands. The box. I looked in the trash can for the empty box that the pregnancy test had come in. The one that I'd thrown away.

Huh?

It wasn't there either.

Where is it?

I headed to check my top drawer.

I'd had the pregnancy test hidden under my bras and panties for a few days before taking it, hoping that I would get lucky and my period would finally show up, but it never did.

After throwing my underwear in every direction, finally, I came across the unopened box that contained the pregnancy test.

What?

I opened the box just to be sure that the pregnancy test was still inside. It was; still in the wrapper, untouched and unused.

So it was all a dream?

But it'd felt so real.

I touched the back of my neck and my shoulders. I didn't feel sore from where I'd thought Polo had done something to cause me to pass out. Instinctively, I looked in the mirror to check for bruising or something just in case.

Nope. Nothing.

For some reason the smell of flowers seemed to follow me but other than that, all of the evidence pointed towards Eddie's statement.

I'd had one hell of a bad dream!

Oh thank goodness!

Still feeling uneasy, I took a deep breath and exhaled loudly. I looked towards my bedroom window and realized that it was a lot later than I remembered.

It was dark outside and glancing at the clock on the wall, I must have been asleep for hours. But for the life of me, I couldn't remember falling asleep at all. I couldn't seem to sort out my thoughts or even remember what I'd been doing before I'd dozed off.

When did I go to sleep?

The only thing I seemed to remember was my dream.

After sitting down for only a minute or so, I steadied my heartbeat, put my thoughts on stand-by and pulled myself together. The sound of the kids caused me to head in their direction. I inspected them, although I knew that they were fine.

I even quizzed the oldest, but he hadn't been much help.

He only said that he was hungry and asked if he was staying home or going back with Eddie.

A few minutes later, I headed back downstairs to Eddie, who was still sitting in the same spot as though he'd been waiting for me.

"Sorry about that. I must have fallen asleep waiting on you guys. I had a horrible dream."

Eddie looked at me.

"Yeah. You were dreaming about Polo. You were saying his name when I walked in," Eddie said disappointed.

"Trust me, it wasn't a good thing. He was trying to kill me…I think," I shook my head.

Surprisingly, Eddie chuckled.

"Um, well, it was definitely a dream then if he was "trying"."

Huh?

Where the hell did that comment come from?

"What is that supposed to mean Eddie?"

He seemed to be surprised that he'd actually let the remark slip out of his mouth but he had. And he couldn't take it back.

"Nothing. You know Polo is into all of those crime shows and stuff, I'm sure he could pull something off if he wanted too," Eddie said, but I wasn't buying it. That wasn't what he'd meant by his comment, but I didn't say anything.

Polo was into stuff like that, but Eddie was referring to something else. Something more.

"But speaking of Polo, I talked to him about bothering you."

"And?"

"And I told him that you saw something that you weren't supposed to see. And you heard something that you weren't supposed to hear."

I became uncomfortable and I put my guard up just in case my dream was about to come true.

"And?"

"And he said just what I'd thought that he would say. First he said that you were nosey, and then he said that he would back off. You know, people always say that eventually what's done in the dark comes to the light, but the truth is, some secrets are meant to stay hidden Sassi. And some people are willing to do anything to make sure that things stay that way. Some things truly are better off not knowing."

"Meaning?"

"Meaning the problem is solved. Believe me, Polo won't bother you again. I'm sure of it. Unless you want him to...do you?" Eddie asked.

I looked at him.

"Do I what?"

"Do you want Polo to keep bothering you? Are you telling me one thing but showing him another?"

"Well…"

There was that time that I'd given myself to Polo because I was angry at Eddie and the other time because I'd broken into his house and needed a cover-up, so I guess my actions didn't exactly match my words a time or two.

But I knew what was in my heart and what was in my heart was more important than what happened in between my legs when I got near Polo these days.

Sex was good; but love and a life of contentment was better.

I realize that now. I realized that Eddie and my kids, our love and marriage was what was important. Even if I had to by a whole damn box of Polo's little sex toys, my heart just wanted my life with Eddie back.

And that little dream that I'd just had definitely had my mind now on the bigger picture. That could have easily been my reality with all of the reckless things that I'd been doing lately. But since it was just a dream, now I could get back to my plan of trying to win Eddie back.

"It would be too soon if I never saw him again," I said to Eddie with reassurance.

Eddie eyed me for a second.

"Was I not good to you?"

"Yes you were."

"Did I not love you enough? Was I doing something wrong?"

"No Eddie. It wasn't you. Honestly. It was me. If I could take it all back, I would. I promise you. I really would."

"Yeah, but you can't."

Eddie cleared his throat and then he stood up and appeared to be preparing to leave.

I still didn't like how strange I felt inside. I couldn't put my finger on it but something just didn't feel right. Something made me feel like there was something that was right in front of my eyes, but I just couldn't see it. Remembering parts of the dream, there was one thing that I thought that I could ask Eddie. Just to hear his response. Just to see his face.

"Eddie who is Vanessa?" I figured that it was no harm in asking, just to be sure.

"Who? I don't know anyone named Vanessa. Why? Who is she?"

I studied is face. He didn't seem uncomfortable or as if he was trying too hard to appear at ease. He seemed to be telling the truth. Well, at least I asked. I shook my head.

"Nothing."

I took a deep breath.

Wait a minute...what's that smell?

I sniffed the air. I hadn't noticed it before but I damn sure noticed it now.

The scent of Polo's cologne was in the air; the only kind that he ever wore.

So wait, Polo had been here?

Eddie walked by me and my nose automatically recognized that the scent of Polo was on him.

"Why do you smell like Polo?"

"Do I?" Eddie sniffed his shirt.

"I was around him for a while today, maybe the scent rubbed off on me. The boys played with his kids while he and I talked about you. But like I said, he and I had a long conversation and he shouldn't bother anymore."

Well, I guess that was a good enough reason, and I personally knew it to be true. If you were close to Polo for only a few minutes, you were bond to leave his presence smelling like him. I sniffed my own shirt. I still smelled like flowers. I tried to think of which perfume it was, but I couldn't recall any of them smelling like flowers.

"Anything else before I go?" Eddie asked.

"Eddie would you ever hurt me? I mean really hurt me?"

"What? No. Why are you asking me that? For what you and Polo did to me, I should have and to be honest, I wanted to, especially when you called me his name during sex. Now that really pissed me off Sassi. But no matter how much I want to hate you, I can't. You're the mother of my kids. The only woman I've touched over in the last decade. And no matter what, I'll always love you. So, no, I would never hurt you. Our boys need you. I know what you heard on the tape, but it was nothing. I didn't mean it. I was upset. I was angry. I'm in a better place now, mentally and emotionally. It is what it is Sassi."

I knew Eddie well enough to know that he was being sincere. And even if he wasn't, I didn't have a choice but to take his word for it. So, I had to shake away whatever it was that I was feeling and get focused.

It was all a dream.

I said that over and over again in my head a few times. The pregnancy test hadn't been taken or even opened. Looking at my phone call log, I hadn't even called Micki, at all that day, so I really must have been dreaming. So now, I was just going to stay far away from Polo and according to Eddie, he was going to stay away from me too. I was going to focus on Eddie, and not to mention the twenty million dollars that depended on us working things out. I definitely couldn't forget about that.

"Eddie, stay for a little while."

He looked at me.

"I can't."

"Why?"

"If you must know, I have a date," he said, half smiled and walked out the door.

Oh really? I headed to the door and screamed behind him.

"With who Eddie?"

"Now that Sassi, is none of your business," he said.

Like hell it isn't!

I slammed the door at the end of his remark. I stood by the window and watched Eddie get into the car.

Who told him that he could go out on a date? If I wasn't dating, he sure as hell wasn't dating either! Sure I'd messed up. But even I deserved a second chance, and some way, somehow, I was going to get Eddie give me one.

I wasn't going to make him take me back; whether it was for the love and for the money.

"Date my ass, we will see about that mister," I mumbled as I grabbed my purse and my keys from the living room table. I wasn't going to let him move on without a fight.

"Kids! Come on! We got a date to ruin!" I yelled and waited impatiently for them to scurry down the stairs.

~***~

Being married to Eddie for all of those years sure came in handy. I knew exactly where he would take his date, and he was beyond furious when the kids and I showed up at the restaurant. I was as bold as ever, and I walked right up to their table and the kids and I took a seat. I introduced myself as his wife and made sure that the tiny woman understood that I was prepared to be the baby mama from hell if she even thought that she and Eddie were about to have something going on. If she wanted to date Eddie, then she was going to also be dating me too.

It's safe to say that she wasn't too fond of my approach, and that Eddie had a little too much baggage than she was willing to accept and more drama than she'd signed up for.

Before they even brought out her food, she was gone. I don't think I have ever seen Eddie so mad, our entire marriage, than he was that night. Well, except for when he found out about the affair between Polo and I. He was so upset that it was almost funny.

He'd even kicked me and stepped on my toes a few times under the table before his date finally became uncomfortable and left. But I didn't care. I'd gotten what I'd wanted out of the deal.

I'd ruined his date.

Boom!

But since that day, Eddie had been letting me have it. He was fussing and cussing, every chance that he could about my behavior. He was constantly reminding me that I was the cause of our divorce, but he didn't have to remind me of that.

I knew that already. The point is that I was trying to fix it and make it right. But Eddie wasn't planning on making it easy.

"Hey Eddie."

"Hey Stupid," Eddie said trying to start an argument, but I wasn't falling for it this time. I was trying to get back on his good side.

"Okay, well can I be Mrs. Stupid and you be Mr. Stupid and we get stupid married, again, and live stupid-happily-ever after?" I tried to make a joke.

"Keep stupid-dreaming," Eddie said dryly.

I tried to keep myself from laughing at his little attempt to be mad at me.

"Okay. So, what time are you coming to get the boys?"

I wanted to know how much time I had. I wanted to be done cooking Eddie's favorite dinner so that he could have a chance to eat before taking the kids for the night. And I wanted to have time to get all dolled up so that I could remind him of what he was missing.

"I'll be there."

Eddie hung up without saying goodbye.

"Bastard!" I screamed at the phone before slamming it down. I couldn't help but chuckle. Eddie trying to be mad was just a tad bit cute.

"Knock, Knock," Micki chimed, walking in with her bad ass kids, my niece included.

I had been distant from her since having the dream. It wasn't intentionally. But I'm sure she'd noticed.

"I've been calling you."

"I know. I've been so busy. And I've just had a lot on my mind lately."

"Um huh. You want to talk about it?"

"No. Not really. It isn't important."

"What is it? Oh no, you're pregnant."

"Girl no. I'm not pregnant."

That's right. I wasn't pregnant. So I had definitely just been dreaming. I hadn't even needed to take the pregnancy test. My period started later on that same night after fussing with Eddie for hours on end about my stunt at the restaurant. And to date, it was one of the worst periods that I'd ever had! I mean I was bleeding through my clothes and everything.

It had me wanting to sleep with my ass up in the air just so I didn't mess up my sheets. That's just how bad it was. I figured that it had been late due to stress and I could only assume that stress was playing a part with how heavy it was as well. But if it didn't slow up soon, I was going to the hospital or something because it was becoming a bit much to handle.

Hell, I was just glad that I wasn't pregnant.

"Well, that's good. One less problem you have to worry about."

"Yeah. I guess so.

"So, I met someone," Micki chimed.

"He isn't white is he?" I joked.

"Actually he is. How did you know that? Who told you?"

Wait…what?

Okay, now this was freaking me out!

Of course prior to having the "dream" or even that day, I had told Micki about my possibly pregnant status. She was my best friend. Of course she knew. But we hadn't talked, so I hadn't told her anything about my dream as of yet or that she'd said those exact words to me in it.

Something was wrong. Something was very wrong.

I stared at her.

"Why you looking at me like that? What's wrong with you?" Micki questioned. "I know. I've always said that I wouldn't date a white man but time is money…literally."

Micki laughed and started messing with the things that I had on the counter. She was sneaking and tasting whatever she could.

She giggled, knowing that I was about to stop her.

Hmmm…

She seemed normal. Maybe I was thinking about it all too much. Maybe it was just a coincidence. It had to be because if I hadn't been dreaming, I would be pregnant.

I wasn't pregnant.

I was bleeding more than a patient having open heart surgery in between my legs and I'd never even taken the pregnancy test.

I shook my head.

"So what about this man?"

"What other than he's a sexy, tall glass of milk? He's older too. Like ten years or so. But I like his maturity. He's divorced. Three kids. Professional. Smart. And from the conversations that we've had, he seems to be a little on the freaky side too," Micki proclaimed.

Okay, so this white man was different from the one that she'd explained to me in my dream.

Good.

"I need that money Sassi. For me and my babies. Hell, I need love too. But I would love twenty million dollars, you know. I gotta' make him fall in love with me. So, for starters, I need you to teach me how to cook. I'm a little challenged in the kitchen as you know," she laughed.

She was right.

If it wasn't fried chicken or something simple, in a box or in a bag, Micki couldn't cook it.

"I'll see what I can do."

"You might as well. You have plenty of time to teach me now. I mean, you don't have a husband or a man on the side anymore…right? And you're unemployed. What else do you have to do?" Micki started to laugh hysterically and I punched her in the arm.

"Sorry. Too soon?"

"Yes. Way too soon," I growled although she was absolutely right. I'd lost everything. But I was going to get it back. Just watch me.

We chatted for a while longer and then she headed out. Just as she pulled off, Eddie pulled up. I checked myself in the mirror.

Damn it! I looked a mess. I wanted to be dressed before he came by.

"How are you going to catch a man, looking like a man?" I scowled my reflection, and threw off my scarf just before Eddie turned the knob.

"Hey," I chimed.

Eddie walked in without speaking.

He smelled like Polo again.

So, what they were all buddy-buddy again, while I had to work for it? What kind of crap was that? If anything, he should have been equally mad at the both of us. I mean to me that made more sense.

They'd always been close but damn! You'd think that he would have been more concerned with trying to mend the relationship with the woman that he'd married and the mother of his kids, rather than mending his friendship with the man that was just as guilty. Hell if he wanted a best friend that bad, I could be his best friend, and his wife, and I was the one with that good stuff that had been making him cum in just two minutes for the last few years.

Humph. I'm just saying.

More than ever before, their friendship made me feel some kind of way. They'd always been too close for comfort, but at that moment I realized that maybe they'd been close in an unhealthy sort of way. It was more than just some "we grew up together" bull crap. They could tell that to someone else who might actually believe it because as of that very moment, I no longer did.

Yet, I didn't say anything since I was trying to get on Eddie's good side and didn't want to argue.

I continued to sniff him as he sniffed the air.

"You made chicken and dumplings didn't you?"

I nodded.

"Are the boys ready to go?"

"Not quite. You want a plate?"

"No. I'm fine."

"Stop being a jackass. Come on. It's your favorite," I said heading to the kitchen. I knew that the peer pressure from his stomach was going to make him follow me. I looked behind me and smiled as he entered the kitchen and took a seat as I fixed his plate.

Once he started to dig in, I started to talk.

"So how are you?"

"I'm fine Sassi. We talk every day. You know that already."

Ugh! I swear I wanted to haul off and smack him.

"I'm just making conversation Eddie. You don't have to be so mean and nasty with me dang. Why are you acting like that?"

"Like what?"

"Like you hate me or something."

Eddie didn't respond.

"It's not fair."

He sat the fork down and looked at me.

"Fair? Please don't go there. Life ain't fair. And love damn sure ain't fair. Adultery ain't fair. Betrayal ain't fair. Adultery ain't fair. Should I keep going?"

"Should I curse you the hell out?"

Eddie snickered at my comment.

"How come you act like you hate me but not Polo? He was wrong too."

"And I know that Sassi."

"But you aren't acting like it. You two are hanging out and being friendly while I'm here trying to figure out how to convince you to come back to me. I'm trying to figure out how to show you that I made a terrible mistake. But yet you are letting Polo off the hook as though he wasn't involved."

"How do you figure that we are hanging out?"

"Because you are. Are you telling me that you're not? Have you seen him again lately? Other than that day that you said that you talked to him about me?"

"No."

"Then why do you smell just like him again Eddie?"

Eddie picked up his fork and took a bite of his food.

He swallowed and continued eating.

"So, you were around him?"

"Didn't I tell you that I don't want to discuss Polo with you? Ever? I did what I told you I would do. I told him to leave you alone. There's nothing else to talk about concerning Polo with you. Period. You screwed my best friend Sassi. What don't you get?"

"And I said that I was sorry."

"Sorry isn't good enough."

"But it's a start."

"There's a start. But there's also a finish. You chose our finish. I didn't."

"Well, I'm choosing to start again then."

"Sorry, I've dropped out of the race."

"Then get your ass back in it."

"No. I don't want to."

"You don't mean that."

"Yes. I do."

No he didn't. I was sure of it. Eddie still loved me even if he didn't want to and even if he was trying to deny it.

"So let me ask you something. Polo has always done what he's wanted to do so why would he listen to you now about not bothering me?"

"Like I told you, he doesn't want any more problems on top of the ones that he already has. And neither do you," Eddie said.

"What does that mean Eddie?"

"Nothing."

"It means something. What did you mean by that Eddie?"

"Let's just say that you only know the side of Polo that you need to know."

You mean there was a whole other side to his craziness? Was that even possible? If Polo could be any worse than he already was, I definitely didn't want to know what his other side was like.

"So what he has some other side?"

"Don't we all?"

"I don't."

"Yes you do. Your other side is a slut."

Okay, now if I smacked the crap out of him I would be wrong right?

"Sorry. I shouldn't have said that."

"If calling me names makes you feel better, call me names Eddie. Get it all out. And then forgive me and let's move on from this."

"I do forgive you."

"No you don't. You're just saying that because it sounds good, but we both know that you don't really forgive me. So, stop lying Eddie."

Eddie stood up, without finishing his food and walked out of the kitchen. I could tell that he was frustrated and maybe even on the defense. But why was the question.

"Why don't you want to forgive me?"

"I said I do."

"But you're lying. Why won't you truly forgive me Eddie?

"Would you forgive me if I was the one that had cheated on you?"

"It isn't like you haven't before."

"That was before we were married and it meant nothing."

"Still. You slept with my best friend too. So that makes us even Eddie."

"No. It doesn't. Not at all."

Eddie looked at me but it was as though he couldn't give me eye contact. As though looking me in the eyes made him nervous or uncomfortable.

"What is it that you aren't telling me Eddie?"

He screamed for the boys and they hurried down the stairs.

"Nothing."

"Yes there is. What is it?"

"I said nothing."

Either it was me or Eddie was definitely different.

Despite messing up his date, his talk, his tone, his face expressions, everything about him was just different.

Maybe he was enjoying being unattached a little too much which meant that I needed to work a little faster with getting him back.

"What are you hiding Eddie? Why can you truly forgive Polo but not me? What is it between you two huh? What does he know about you that I don't know?"

"What? Sassi. Please. I don't know what is going on with you lately but maybe I should keep the boys with me and my folks until you figure it out."

"No. I'm fine."

"Could've fooled me."

"I just want you back Eddie."

"No Sassi. Just no."

"Why?"

"Because I don't want to be with you Sassi, okay? I don't know how I could be with you, or how I could touch you, without thinking about him touching you too."

"I'm sorry Eddie. I really am."

Eddie opened the front door and the boys went outside. He looked back at me.

"I'll keep the boys until Saturday. Clear your head. Pull yourself together. And go to the doctor, please," Eddie said, nodding down at my white pants.

I glanced down.

Ugh! Not again! There was blood on the front and the back of my pants. I hadn't even felt it seeping through.

Eddie and the boys walked off and I headed to clean myself up so that I could go to the hospital. Apparently, I couldn't put it off any longer.

An hour or so later, I was walking into the hospital.

It was crowded as usual and I was glad that I put on two pads, plus a tampon just in case it took a while for them to get to me. I would be extremely embarrassed if I had an accident in public.

"Is this seat taken?"

She looked at me but she didn't say anything so I sat down.

She coughed but she didn't cover her mouth.

Nasty ass heffa'!

I looked at her with disgust but she grinned.

"Girl, don't worry. What I got, you can't get. At least not by a cough anyway."

The sound of my name over the intercom caused me to smack my lips because I had to get right back up and head back to the registration desk. The nurse asked me a few more questions and as she typed, I stared off into the distance.

Wait…is that Polo?

The man was walking back out the door and I couldn't see his face but I knew that it was him. From his walk, to the way that he was dressed and from the hair that was peeking out from underneath the fitted cap that he was wearing.

Um huh. He was going to stay away from me my ass!

Eddie should have known that Polo was just telling him what he'd wanted to hear. Even I knew how obsessive Polo could be and that he would always find a way to do whatever he wanted to do.

I headed back to take a seat and instead of taking my seat next to the woman, I sat in a now empty seat about three seats away from her. Even though I tried not to look at her, I found it hard not to stare at her.

She was gorgeous; she had strong, but charmingly cute features. She was very attractive and she was overdressed. I wasn't sure which brand or label she was wearing but she simply looked like money so I knew that she was wearing something expensive and something that I probably couldn't even pronounce.

But as she coughed again, I was reminded that looks can be deceiving.

"Is Sassy your real name?" she spoke loud enough for me to hear her.

"Yes. It's Sassi…with an "I"."

"Oh, well Sassi with an "I", I'm Carmen with a "K". Nah, I'm lying. It's with a C. Sassi sounds like a name one of my girls should have used back in the day."

"Your girls?"

"Yes. I was a pimp," she laughed.

Okay, was this some kind of joke?

"Well, actually more like a madam. And I was a darn good one too. I knew how to make that money and I had girls that didn't mind making it with me. Good times. Those were the days I tell you," she said it as though what she was saying was normal.

"You had um, prostitutes?" I said almost in a whisper being that there were other people around.

"Lots of them. Expensive ones too. Only they weren't called prostitutes. But in reality, that's exactly what they were. I used to work for this hotel; well, everyone at this hotel used to work for me. If you had the right assets, I could get you paid. Anyway, not anymore. That ship has sailed."

She started to cough and it took a while for her to get herself together.

Though I was disturbed, I couldn't help but be curious.

"You stopped because you're sick?"

"No. Other reasons. Funny. When I was doing what I wanted nothing ever happened. And by that I mean screwing every Tom, Dick or Harry, that I wanted to. But as soon as I tried to live the normal life; you know all of that settling down, one man and one woman type of thing, again, I ended up paying for my past mistakes; more or less anyway."

Just from what she was saying, I automatically knew her diagnosis.

"My knight in shining armor, turned out to be nothing more than a devil in a suit. He gave me the one thing that I can't pay to get rid of. HIV. Lots of folks thought I had it a long time ago, but I didn't. There was a rumor, once, that'd I'd gotten it from a man that raped me years ago, but that was wrong. I'd gotten it from a man that I'd trusted. One that I'd actually found a way to give my heart to despite all I'd been through. I guess it was just my fate. Everyone has to pay for their sins in some way. I guess this is the way that I have to pay for mine."

She sounded sad, but she didn't look sad. She was actually somewhat grinning or maybe her beauty just made it hard for me to see her without being in awe.

I was surprised that she was sharing her life story with me. I was a complete stranger but I guess she figured that she didn't have anything else to lose. Or maybe she just wanted to get some things off of her chest. Either way, my nosey self was all ears, listening and I had no plans on stopping her.

"What about you?"

"Oh no, I'm just having some stomach problems. That's all."

"Are you married?" she asked.

"I was. Unfortunately, I'm recently divorced."

She looked at me for a while.

"And it was your fault wasn't it? You had an affair didn't you?" she asked.

"How did you know?"

"I just do. It's written all over your face. Chile, there is nothing out here in these streets except for what I have and people like me."

"Meaning?"

"It's not worth stepping out on your marriage, especially if you find a man that actually isn't trying to step out on you first. These married men that I come into contact with lately are ridiculous. They could care less about their wives, but you running around here stepping out on one that was faithful. Am I right?" I nodded as she chastised me in a tone as though she'd known me forever. And for some reason, from her, I received the message differently than I ever had before.

I heard her loud and clear.

I was wrong. I never should have cheated on Eddie, especially not with his best friend or a man like Polo.

That could be me in her shoes.

"I tell you, these men are a mess. I have one married guy that calls and bothers me more than the law should allow. I ask him all the time, like dude, where in the hell is your wife? Straight foolishness."

"And he knows about your status?"

She laughed in a crazy way.

"He thinks that he can have his cake and eat it too. But he's eating more than cake when he's in between my legs. He's eating that positive HIV status too. But it serves him right. He knew before he pursued me that he already had a wife. I didn't know until afterwards. Honestly. And though she's innocent, I blame her too. Because he comes to get from me, what his wife just won't do. One messed up marriage if you ask me. And that was even before I came into the mix."

She waited for my response but I didn't say anything. I didn't know what to say.

"All I'm saying is, sex, a piece of meat, comes a dime a dozen. You can get some wood from a man when you can't even get him to buy you a sandwich. Ask him for a burger, and there's a fifty percent chance that you will get an excuse. But ask him for some dick. Chile he will be there before you can even hang up the phone."

I hadn't dated in a while, but I was sure that she knew what she was talking about.

"Good men are hard to find, Sassi with an "I". If you are lucky enough to find one, you hold on to them with everything that you got. Do you still love him?"

I nodded.

"Are you sorry?"

I nodded again.

"Would you do it again?"

I shook my head no.

"Then fix it. If there's still room to fix it, take it from me, fix it. Any man that doesn't cheat is worth fighting for. If he's faithful and loyal, you can get through anything else. Didn't your mother ever teach you anything? Mine sure as hell didn't. But life did."

The nurse called Carmen and she got up. She didn't say anything else, and she didn't even bother to glance back at me. She simply followed the nurse and disappeared.

Though she deserved some kind of prison sentence or something for what she was handing out, I couldn't help but think that maybe she was some kind of guardian angel of mine or something. She'd just made me see things clearer than I ever had before. She'd said exactly what I needed to hear and now, more than ever, it was important for me to get things back on track with Eddie.

I just had to figure out how.

"Where are you?" I answered Mama's call.

"At the hospital."

"What? What's wrong? What happened? I'm on my way."

"Mama no. I'm fine. I'm just having a really bad, heavy period and I'm here to get it checked out."

"Oh," Mama exhaled.

Dang. She'd acted like I was a breath away from death or something. Mama said something to someone in the background and then she said something to me.

"Well, let me know when you leave."

"Where you at Mama?"

"I'm at home why?"

"Who are you talking to?"

Mama didn't say anything at first.

"Why?"

"I just asked Mama."

"Well, you worry about what you got going on there. I'll call and check on you later," she said and hung up.

She was just so rude!

After hanging up with Mama, I put my phone on silent and just sat there in my thoughts. I thought about Eddie and I thought about the kids. I even thought about Polo.

Finally after another thirty minutes or so, it was finally time for me to see what was going on with my good stuff.

"Well Mrs...."

"It's Ms. For now anyway. I haven't updated my insurance cards."

"Excuse me. Well, what you are experiencing is a miscarriage. The hcg levels are still very present in your lab results. You were pregnant. The bleeding is a result of you losing the baby. We're going to take a look just to make sure everything is going through the proper process. By chance do you know about how far along you were?"

I was pregnant? A miscarriage?

Well…there is a God! That was nothing but luck right there. I felt terrible for being so happy about the news but that baby wouldn't have been anything but trouble. If I'd had the baby, all hell would have surely broken loose if it was Polo's and not Eddie's. There would have been no way in hell that Eddie would have ever forgiven me for having a baby by his best friend.

"No. Not exactly."

"That's fine. We will just take a quick look. And then you will be on your way. It's a process and you will have to see it all the way through to the end. We can give you something for discomfort. I'm sorry for your loss."

I'm not.

I spent the next two hours getting checked out and counting my blessings. I wouldn't have had a clue as to who the father would have been but I no longer had to worry about it.

It was all good. And it was my little secret. And I wasn't telling anyone. Not even big mouthed Micki.

Walking out of the hospital, I headed for my car but immediately I spotted his car.

Polo's.

His car was facing in the opposite direction but I was sure that he was staring at me out of his rearview mirror.

He must have followed me to the hospital.

Just as I reached for the door handle, his car started and he pulled off. I guess this was his way of keeping his word to Eddie, but still satisfying his need to be Polo.

But you know what?

I didn't care if he watched me from afar; as long as he kept his distance and as long as he left me alone.

I was baby-free and now my only focus was getting my husband back. Thanks to the woman from the hospital, I was focused and nothing was going to keep me from trying everything that I could to make Eddie fall back in love with me.

And I needed Polo as far away from the situation to make that possible.

I got into the car to find that there were roses on my passage seat. I really needed to remember to lock my doors. I was sure that Polo had put them there. As I drove down the street, I threw the roses out the window and I entertained my thoughts.

There just had to be a way to get rid of Polo for good.

But how?

I didn't have a clue.

****

Chapter 2

"Hey Mama," I rubbed my eyes as I turned away from the door and she walked inside.

"Look at that booty. Your Mama gave you that chile," she commented.

Immediately I became uncomfortable because I was still gaining weight, although I was barely even eating.

"I thought I told you to call me when you left the hospital that day."

"I forgot."

She looked around the house as I sat on the couch.

"You need to clean up."

"Tell me about it. Or better yet, could you clean up for me?"

"Those days are long gone. Where are the kids?"

"Still with Eddie."

"Are you and Eddie…"

"No Ma. He still hates me."

"Of course he does. Well, he doesn't hate you. He hates your loose booty as he called it," Mama laughed.

"Not funny Mama."

She continued to chuckle as I pouted.

"Oh yes it is. But trust your Mama. He still loves you. Chile, ten plus years of love doesn't go away overnight or even in a few weeks or months. And real love surely doesn't go away just because you're angry or because you want it to. You just have to make him remember. Make him remember why he fell in love with you in the first place. Make him fall in love with you again."

"You make it sound so easy. And funny, you didn't try this approach with Daddy," I teased knowing that my comment was going to get under her skin.

"Your father was a…let's not go there. He didn't deserve my love and after a while, I no longer wanted his. But you and Eddie are different. You both still love each other."

I rolled my eyes.

"So, you're here…what is it?"

"Um, nothing. I just came by because you didn't call me."

Yeah right.

"So you're pregnant ain't you? That's why them hips spreading like that. How far along?"

"I lost it Mama. And please don't tell anyone. I wasn't even going to tell you."

"You didn't have to. I already knew. A mother knows sweetie. Was it Eddie's? Or Polo's?" Mama frowned as she asked the question.

I shrugged.

"I don't know. And I don't care. I'm only happy that it's gone."

"Yes, because that surely would have started World War III."

"Honey you don't have to tell me. And I mean it, don't say anything to anybody Mama. Not even Eddie. You know how you tend to forget that you are my Mama, and not his."

"I don't forget. I just wanted you to do right, that's all. And I won't say anything. You have my word."

Mama got extremely quiet for a second too long. I could tell that something was on her mind and I waited patiently for her to finally say it.

"Did I ever tell you about the conversation between Patrice and I? Before she died?"

At the mention of Patrice's name, I sat up straight and gave my mother my full attention. There wasn't a day that went by that I didn't think about Patrice. No matter what, she had been like a sister to me, and no matter how angry I was at her for not telling me that she'd slept with Eddie, I loved her and I wished we'd had those last moments to reconcile. I wished that she'd told me that she was sick.

"At the hospital right? What about her?"

"Uh, yeah. There was more between her and your father other than the lie that she told wasn't it?"

I looked at Mama. I mean, there wasn't anything that she could do to ether one of them now. They were both dead. I might as well go ahead and tell her the truth.

"Yes."

Mama waited on me to finish my sentence.

"Patrice and Daddy had an affair Mama. She didn't only lie on him, but years later, they started sleeping together. And there's something else. She even got pregnant by him and she had an abortion by him."

Mama cringed and I could tell by her facial expression that she was as hot as hen piss by the truth. But I could also tell by her breathing that the truth had hurt her, whether she wanted it to or not.

"Wait a minute. Didn't Patrice tell you the whole truth? At your hospital visit before she died?"

Mama shook her head.

"No. When I saw her, she just apologized and I assumed it was about the lie. She talked in circles and she didn't even mention any of the other stuff, but I knew there was something more. I'd known for years that your father was screwing somebody. That somebody just happened to be her. I started to think about it the other day, and I figured that I would ask you."

Hell I was surprised that anyone would have wanted my Daddy and his drunk ass. He disgusted me. Even though I'd found out that Patrice had lied on him and had hated him for years for nothing, even though he wasn't a pervert, he was still a drunk. And the worst kind at that.

And of all people, I was surprised that Patrice had even allowed my Daddy to even look at her, let alone touch her. She was so stuck-up, and uppity, so it really didn't make much sense to me.

I shivered in pure disgust.

Ugh.

My phone started to vibrate and I saw that it was a private call. Of course I automatically assumed that it was Polo so I ignored it as Mama continued to talk.

"I sure hope that she's somewhere in hell, burning, right beside your father. They both deserve it."

Mama seemed to dwell on her statement for a second, and then she started talking again.

"So, what did Patrice do with all of her money? She didn't have kids or a man to leave it to," Mama said as though she was making fun of her.

"She left some to me. And to Micki.

"Oh really? How much did she leave you?"

"Twenty million dollars."

"For real?"

"Yes. But it comes with stipulations."

"What kind of stipulations?"

"It's not important."

There was no point in mentioning the guidelines for receiving the money. As much as Mama loved Eddie, she would have been trying her best to force us back together so I could receive my share of the money.

Wait…

That might not be a bad thing since Eddie respected her and her opinion. Maybe things would go smoother with Mama whispering in his ear on my behalf.

"Well Mama since you asked…"

~***~

Talking to the woman at the doctor had really changed my way of looking at things with Eddie. I had to follow my heart, and not to mention that my heart would lead me to more money than I would probably be able to spend in a lifetime.

With Mama now onboard, I was cooking up scheme after scheme to *wow* Eddie and make him fall in love with me again. After all, the woman that was one cough away from her death had a point. If a man loyal and faithful then everything, anything else, could be fixed.

So I was going to fix it.

My phone vibrated again with a private call

That was the third one that day.

I looked at it and so did Eddie but he didn't say anything about it. I knew that it was Polo and he probably figured that it was too.

"What did the doctor's say?" Eddie asked.

"Nothing. They assume that it's just backed up from it being late for a little while."

"It was? Your period? When was it late?"

"A while ago. The doctor said that it was probably a result of stress. No worries. Everything is fine," I lied.

"Oh," Eddie said.

He attempted to leave but I grabbed his arm. He looked at me as if to say stop touching him but he just stood there. I stared at him as though I was trying to get him to see the love that I still had for him in my eyes, but it only seemed to make him uneasy.

"Eddie."

"What?"

"Make love to me. One time."

Eddie looked at me.

"That wouldn't be a good idea."

I ignored his comment and came closer to him.

He didn't move away so I knew that meant that in some way he wanted me too. Slowly, my lips made their way closer and closer to his and just as I puckered up my lips, a car horn wailed and scared us both half to death.

Eddie stepped back.

"I gotta' go."

What?

He opened the door and I watched him head down the sidewalk…to Polo's car.

He got in and hurriedly they drove away.

Bullshit at its finest!

He was in the car with Polo?

Why?

I found my phone and called Polo, but he didn't answer. I was sure that was him that had called me private only minutes ago, but he still sent my call to the voicemail.

I threw my phone on the couch and folded my arms.

Who did they think that they were fooling?

Best friends huh?

There was something more going on between Polo and Eddie. There was something that they were keeping from me or maybe I had just been too blind to see it all of these years until now.

Either way, I was going to find out just what it was.

Even if I had to sleep with Polo again to do it.

~***~

"You asked Eddie to talk to me about "harassing" you, but then you show up at my house," Polo said and turned and walked away from the door.

I sniffed the air.

Um huh, Eddie had definitely smelled like Polo's cologne lately, every single time that he came by the house to be exact.

"His talk obviously didn't work because I know that it has been you calling my phone private again Polo. And I saw you that day that I went to the hospital."

"I don't know what you're talking about Sassi," Polo said behind him.

"Yeah, I bet you don't. Polo, we need to talk."

He sat on the couch and I sat in a chair across from him.

Being there was a bad idea. I knew it. I could feel it.

But I was on a mission. Something just didn't seem right.

It didn't seem normal for their friendship to be able to bounce back after what we'd done yet Eddie was giving me such a hard time. There just had to be more.

"Talk about what Sassi? Me, you and that pus---"

"Ah!" I screamed before he could finish his sentence.

Polo started to laugh.

"Look at him. He knows that you're here," Polo nodded down at his swelling penis.

I didn't want to look, but my eyes looked without my permission. I almost licked my lips, but my bloody vagina reminded me of all of the trouble Polo and his penis had caused.

"Touch it. You know you want to. I know I want you to," Polo said slyly.

"So, what huh? You're playing some kind of roll with Eddie?"

"I'm not playing anything. I'm just staying away from you like I said that I would."

"Why won't you stay away from Eddie too then?"

"Why would I do that? Like I told you before. We will always be friends Sassi."

"But why? That's what I don't get. Why is it so easy for him to forgive you but so hard for him to forgive me and give us another chance?"

"That's something that you're going to have to ask him Sassi."

"But I'm asking you Polo. Is there something kind of, you know something going on between you and Eddie? Like on a different kind of level or something?"

"Bitch…excuse me. I didn't mean to call you that but I know you aren't trying to ask me if we're gay."

"Well, it seems like,"

"It seems like what? You and I both know that I love pussy and pussy loves me too. Period. Don't ask me no stupid stuff like that. I'm all about the kitty cat. By the way, do yours still get wet when you think about me?"

He was such a jerk.

"I don't think about you. I only think about Eddie."

"Then why are you here?"

"Because I want you to help me get him back."

Polo chuckled.

"I'm serious."

"And why would I do that?"

"Because you love him. And because you love me," I said to Polo softly.

"And what about me? What do I get out of all of this? Can I still hit that on the side?"

"No Polo. That's why we are in this mess now."

"You were supposed to be mine Sassi. We would've been so good together. Hell, Eddie and Patrice would have made a better couple. You should've been mine."

"What? How do you figure that?"

"What?"

"About Patrice and Eddie?"

"It's just my opinion."

"So they messed around more than what I was told?"

"No. But in my opinion, she always had a thing for Eddie. Hell, look at me. I've always had a thing for you. I wouldn't have put it past her. He is my best friend, and I'm in love with his wife. Well, ex-wife. She was your best friend and I'm willing to be that she probably always had a thing for your husband. Maybe she was just better at pretending."

I wondered if Polo was trying to tell me something, without actually telling me. Or if he was just screwing with my head. But Patrice was dead and gone, so I definitely couldn't ask her. And really that didn't even really matter.

"Well, I would like to think that you are wrong. Besides, in her will, she encouraged me to work it out with Eddie. So, if your opinion was right, I'm sure that she wouldn't have made me working it out with Eddie a part of her stipulations in order for me to receive what she left behind for me. If she'd really wanted Eddie for herself, all of those years, she definitely wouldn't have told me to get my husband back. Right?"

"Do I look like a psychic? Dig her up and ask her. But I can tell you this, friends, family, no one, is loyal these days."

"You would know now wouldn't you?"

"Our situation was different. You wouldn't understand. I loved you first."

"No you didn't. You didn't even know me."

"Doesn't mean that I didn't love you. I believe in love at first sight."

"Well, I don't."

"You should. Every time Eddie told me about the phone conversations between you two or every time I would sit beside him as he talked to you, got to know you, and as I coached him to be the man that you needed him to be, I feel for you more and more. Just like he did. But oh well. The problem is that my best friend in the whole world loves the hell out of you. Even now believe it or not. But the even bigger problem is that I still love you too." Polo made sure to add that part.

"Eddie doesn't love me. Not anymore he doesn't."

"Yes he does."

"How do you know that Polo?"

"Because I do."

"He said that to you?"

"He says it every day Sassi."

"Then why does he act like he hates me?"

"Because we both agreed to leave you alone," Polo said and immediately he bit his bottom lip and shook his head.

He hadn't meant to say that part.

"What?"

"Nothing."

"What do you mean you both agreed to leave me alone?"

Polo didn't respond.

What kind of crap was that?

"Are you going to answer my question Polo?"

He shook his head.

"No."

"Why?"

"Because."

Why would Eddie even agree to something like that?

With an attitude, I smacked my lips and stood to leave.

I started to walk away, but Polo stood up and grabbed me from behind.

"I miss you."

"Get off of me Polo."

"I love you and miss you so much Sassi. It's killing me to stay away from you."

"Take your hands off of me. Now!"

"You don't miss me? Not even a little bit?" Polo grinded up against me and knees buckled.

My mind didn't want him.

My heart damn sure didn't want him.

But *she* seemed to be begging, yearning for his touch and a few of his long, forceful strokes.

I was sure that after forcing myself to sleep with Polo the last time that the desire would be gone. But I was wrong.

I was oh so wrong.

"No I don't Polo."

"You're lying."

"No I'm not. Let me go."

"I want you."

"People in hell want ice water, but I can assure you that they don't get what they want either. Now let go of me."

"Don't forget, you came over to my house. I could do something to you, anything to you, and who do you think they are going to believe?"

"Try me."

"Is that an invitation?"

"An invitation to get your ass whooped. Try me."

Polo snickered but he loosened his grip and I turned to face him.

"Who were you and Eddie talking about on the video tape Polo?"

He looked at me.

"Who was it that both of you were talking about? It wouldn't have happened to be someone named Vanessa would it?"

I made sure to throw that part in there just in case.

"What video?"

"The one that Eddie told you that I saw."

Polo looked confused.

"What did you see?"

"The tape."

"What tape?"

Okay.

Was he serious?

Or was he just playing dumb?

"The tape where Eddie said that he would kill me if he found out that I was having an affair. And then he asked you if you could do it. Like you did last time, " I bellowed.

Polo just looked at me.

"Eddie didn't tell me anything about a tape. We talked. We always talk. Once he got over being mad, we talked it out and came to an agreement, so what are you talking about?"

"Eddie told me that he told you what I saw."

"Again what did you see and where?"

"I just told you."

I was so confused.

"You're playing with my head right now aren't you? You and Eddie must be up to something huh?"

"I can assure you that we aren't Sassi. What, are you offended it by our relationship? I told you that it wouldn't change."

"But why is the question? Why?"

"Why would it?"

"You know something on him don't you? No, obviously he knows something on you right?"

Polo looked at me.

"You want to know a secret Sassi?"

"What is it? Tell me."

"Maybe I shouldn't."

"Tell me Polo," I begged and touched his chest.

"Girl, don't be touching on me like that. Unless I can touch you," Polo flirted.

"Polo, please. What's the secret?"

"Okay. I will tell you. But you gotta give me something too."

I rolled my eyes.

"I'm not giving you any ass Polo."

"Okay. Give me a kiss then."

"Why?"

"You give me something. I'll give you something. Kiss me."

Polo came so close to me that I felt like I was about to melt from the warmth of his breath.

It's just a little kiss. Kissing ain't ever hurt nobody.

The problem was that I didn't know if Polo was really going to tell me something after I kissed him.

Polo moved in for a kiss and I allowed his lips to touch mine. And I regretted it as soon as they did. The way that he kissed me sent chills up my spine and it had me wondering where he'd been all of my life. Though he'd always been there, his kiss seemed to make me feel alive.

Complete.

Rejuvenated

And hornier than a mother---

"Okay," I said pulling away from him.

"You felt it too didn't you? I told you. We were meant to be together Sassi. I just know it."

I shook my head.

"Now keep your end of the deal Polo. What secret?"

Polo took a deep breath.

"Look Sassi, Eddie and I are as close as brothers."

"Duh, tell me something I don't know. I was married to him for the last decade. Don't you think I know that?"

"No. You still don't get it."

Polo looked at me.

"Eddie saved my life once. I was only about eight. One day, we were in his parent's backyard. In the pool. Well, Eddie would swim but I was always scared to get in the water. No one ever taught me how to swim so I would only put my feet in or get in if there was an adult present. Eddie had gone into the house to get us a snack and I dropped my ball in the water. I could have waited for him to come back out and get it but I tried to get it out instead. Accidentally, I fell in. I thought it was over for me. I was flapping my arms and trying to stay above the water, but it wasn't working. Finally I gave up. I have no idea where Eddie came from, but just as I was blacking out, I felt someone tugging me. I opened my eyes to him beating on my chest. When he saw me looking at him he smiled and told me that I almost drowned."

"Oh my goodness!"

"Yeah. But strangely, he didn't seem scared at all. It was as though it wasn't a big deal to him. Instead, he handed me my snack and then he said let's keep my accident to ourselves otherwise we wouldn't be able to play near the pool anymore. That was the first secret we ever agreed to keep just between the two of us. The secret of Eddie saving my life."

How touching! So, that's why Polo cared about Eddie the way that he did. Eddie had saved his life. Who knew!

"But there's something else. No one knows this. Not even our parents know that Eddie and I know this."

My heart started beating faster and faster.

Please don't let him say what I thought that he was going to say.

"My mother slept with Eddie's father. There was never any blood test or anything done, but I heard my mother say that it was a strong possibility."

"What? There's a possibility that you and Eddie could really be brothers?"

Polo nodded.

What the hell! Instantly I hoped that they weren't real blood brothers. If that was the case, I would definitely be considered a slut.

"When my mother found out that she was pregnant, she hurriedly married the man that I called Dad until the day that he died, but the truth is she didn't know if he was really my father at all. For all she knew, I could have been the product of Eddie's father's infidelity. She could have had a baby by a married man."

"What? What the hell are you talking about Polo?"

He stared at me intensely.

"This doesn't leave this room. I've said too much already. Eddie would die if he knew that I told you this because we usually keep our secrets just between the two of us. But I'm trying to make a point. My mother used to keep me in the house all the time. I would watch everyone from the window. The other kids playing and all of that other stuff. I think that's why I'm so obsessed with looking and watching people to this day. Even when she worked, she had a sitter that would come and watch me, but I couldn't go outside. I would just watch from the window. Anyway, my parents ended up getting divorced and my mother just became different. As if she didn't care about being found out anymore. That's when I finally started playing with Eddie and the rest is history. Though I didn't discover her secret until years later. And whether or not Eddie's father knows the truth about me or not is still up in the air. Of course we've never asked. They don't even know that we know."

I tried to make sure that I understood him correctly.

"So what you are saying is that you and Eddie really are brothers?"

"Maybe. Maybe not. We secretly just like to think that we are. And there's no point in knowing the truth now. We found out and kept the secret between the two of us. But trust me, there are plenty of more secrets that we share."

"How? How did you find out?"

"Well, Eddie and I used to have this thing were we liked to sneak and listen on the other end of the telephone. One day I picked up the phone and heard a discussion between my mother and my aunt. I heard her confess everything. I heard her say that her neighbor's husband could be my real father. She filled her in on their affair all of those years ago and how she'd blamed her pregnancy on my "dad" so that she wouldn't have to go through the shame of being someone's pregnant mistress, if I really had been Eddie's father's son. She didn't know whether I was or not, but from what she'd said, they had been screwing, Eddie's father and my mother, only a month or so since she'd moved in beside them. The house that I grew up in had been passed down to her from my grandmother. I'm not sure how long Eddie's family had been in the house next door. Anyway, I kept what I'd heard to myself until I was about twelve and then I told Eddie. At that moment we weren't just best friends anymore. We became brothers. And we didn't want our families feuding, fussing and fighting, to tear us apart from each other, so we just said nothing. And we never found out the truth."

I couldn't even reply.

"So as I said, we are closer than you could ever imagine. Every bad thing. Every tear. Every disappointment. And every secret, we share and know about each other. We were there for each other. When we have no one, we've always had each other. He's the only person that I can truly depend on and I just about messed it up. He's the only person that has ever really given a damn about me. And that's for real. That's my brother right there. He's all that I have. So talking about it know, I gotta get my feelings in check and my dick in check. I crossed the line and I know I did. I can't take it back. And between me and you, I don't wish that I could because he knew you were supposed to be mine. I saw you first. I wanted you first. But that's neither here nor there. We talked about it as brothers and the best thing for us both to do is to back off. It's best for both of us to just stop loving you. He left you. I have to live with never having you. We settled it. But we both still love you."

I was flabbergasted with all that he'd revealed so I didn't say anything.

"But Eddie didn't mention anything about a tape. What tape? My tape? How do you know about my tapes? How did you find them? What exactly did you hear?"

Still overwhelmed, I answered him.

"Under your bed Polo; the video tapes that you had on your camcorder. You lied to me. You recorded us having sex and a conversation that you had with Eddie where it almost sounded like he implied that you did something crazy or hurt someone before. I'm not sure if it was for him or on his behalf, or if he just knew about something that you did, but I know what I heard. But I deleted them. All of them."

I was so confused about everything that my head was starting to hurt. Polo had said a mouth full and obviously Eddie hadn't said enough. They were closer than I'd ever imagine and at that moment, I realized that I had been right about Eddie all along.

If he ever had to choose, it wouldn't be me. It would be Polo. And his choice was clearer than ever.

"I let you in, so do me a favor and keep your mouth close. Some secrets are meant to stay hidden."

"Funny, Eddie said the same thing."

"Because it's the truth Sassi. Not everybody can handle the truth. About others. Or about themselves. Sometimes pretending something never happened is the only way. But what's also true is that we both love you. In different ways; nevertheless, but we do. I tried not to feel anything for you for years. I'll take the blame. I messed up. But love is crazy ain't it? Sometimes it just does what it wants and you can't always control it. My love for Eddie overpowered what I felt for you for years, and somehow, not too long ago, my feelings got the best of me and I started giving in to them. I could blame Eddie. I could blame myself for not approaching you. But the only things I'll blame is love."

Love didn't have a thing to do with all of this.

"Run away with me."

"What?"

Polo smirked at me in a devilish kind of way, but I rolled my eyes at him as I opened the front door.

But just as I started to walk away, Polo mumbled.

"Oh and you forgot to check in the other boxes under the sink in my bathroom. I always make copies," he laughed and slammed the door behind me.

Ugh! Pervert!

~***~

"Eddie can we talk?"

I was debating whether or not to keep what Polo told me from Eddie, but it was clear that Eddie would always side with Polo. After all, hell, they might be brothers.

I couldn't help but feel like he should have told me something like that, but of course he hadn't. And he'd never planned to.

But this whole agreeing for both of them to leave me alone crap just didn't work for me. I wanted my life with Eddie back. I was sure that I could probably start dating, and meet someone new, but I didn't want to. I just wanted to fix it. I just wanted Eddie.

"What?"

Eddie seemed so annoyed with me but with what Polo told me, maybe it was all an act. Maybe he did still love me and just didn't want to show it because of their little agreement. Maybe he was just pretending.

Before I spoke again I tried to find the right words.

"I know you are tired of hearing this, but I just have to say this. I have to try to get through to you and tell you how I feel. The least that I can do is try."

"Meaning?"

"Meaning I was wrong Eddie. I know I used to complain about so much but I was wrong. You were all that I'd ever needed and I messed it all up. You weren't the wrong husband at all. I just couldn't see it."

I started to cry. Sure his sex sucked, unless he took a pill. Sure he wasn't exciting anymore or spontaneous, but now it just seemed like those things should have been easy fixes. And he'd tried to fix them, but for some reason for me his attempts hadn't been good enough but they should have been. Had I not done any of this, everything would be fine. None of the extra stuff would have happened. We would have been okay.

So what if I was still horny and sometimes bored?

Being horny and bored was better than this situation any day. There were other options. Options that didn't involve being satisfied by another man.

Eddie just looked at me. He studied me for a while and then he shook his head.

"No Sassi, actually you were right. I'm not the man that you think I am. The truth is…" Eddie stopped.

Oh hell, what was he about to say?

"The truth is that I should have never pursued you. Yes I knew that Polo wanted you, but I came after you anyway."

He waited for a response but I didn't say anything.

"Not to say that I didn't fall in love with you, I did. I loved you and still do love you very much. But back then, Polo seemed to get every woman, and everything. I wouldn't say that I was jealous. I guess I just wanted to see if you would bite. That night after he told me you were the woman that he had been watching, and I do mean watching. Polo has an obsession problem with everything; cologne, people, recording, sex, women. Whatever interests him at the time. But you know that already. But after he told me and the more and more I looked at you, I wondered if boring, responsible me, could get someone like you. Someone that Polo had his eye on. I knew that I was no competition for Polo's charm, so I took advantage of the situation. I knew that for some reason you made him nervous, so I made the first move. When I told him that we exchanged numbers even he couldn't believe it. He was upset. He didn't say it but I know him and I could tell. But I also thought that he would get over it as soon as he found someone else. And for a while he did. Well, at least I thought that he did. But I guess I was wrong. Obviously you had more of an effect on him than I thought that you did."

In a way, I felt betrayed, or like a piece of meat, or a bet gone too far or something. It didn't make what I'd done to Eddie right, but damn he'd only wanted me because Polo had wanted me first.

Bummer.

"So, I was just some contest to you?"

"No, well, maybe in a way at first. But I fell in love with you."

"Before or after you screwed my best friend?" I asked him, referring to Patrice.

"Patrice was one woman that just happened. She had money, but not only was she unattractive, so was her personality. But that seemed to be the women that came my way. You were different. She and I were nothing more than sex. We slept together on the first night and never intended to be anything more; which is why we thought it was best just not to tell you about us. It meant nothing. She meant nothing."

Maybe not to him, but Polo had reason to believe that maybe she'd felt that they should have been much more.

"Sassi, Polo and I have a lot of history. Most of it good but some of it wasn't all that gravy. Every girl I'd ever wanted, he got to her first. Every woman that I'd ever dreamed would be mine; he would screw them and throw them away like trash. But I beat him to you. I got to you first. Maybe he would have been different with you. Maybe you were the one woman that could have changed his ways. You seemed to be the only woman that he even somewhat looked at like a person and not just a piece of ass, but I didn't care about that. I wanted you because he'd wanted you Sassi. So there you have it. So, maybe I deserved for you to cheat on me with him because of what I did. I should have never married you in the first place."

I clutched my chest hoping that it would stop my heart from breaking. I didn't care if he really felt that way, I would never accept that.

"Don't say that."

"But it's true. I brought this on myself. I should have just left you alone, especially since I know how Polo can be. To be honest, I'm surprised he didn't try to make his move on you years ago," Eddie said.

"But I don't care about all of that Eddie. I should have never slept with your best friend. So what if he'd wanted me first, I wanted you."

"No you wanted who he told me to be. You wanted who I was pretending to be. Once I stopped pretending, you got bored. You fell in love with me when I was pretending to be a little like Polo."

"That's not true," I lied.

Maybe he was right but now I was in a different place.

Now I knew that the grass wasn't greener on the other side and I didn't want to walk on anybody's lawn but his.

"I wanted you Eddie. And I still do. Can we start over?"

Eddie shook his head.

Sure Polo said that they both agreed to leave me alone but despite everything, Eddie and I could just start over. I no longer even cared about the sex. I just wanted our life back.

"I don't know Sassi. I really don't know. Maybe we should just leave well enough alone."

I walked closer to him. I laid my head on his chest and waited to see if he would hug me.

He did.

"If I could turn back the hands of time, I would have never done that to you."

"And if I could turn back the hands of time, Sassi, I'm not sure that I would have ever married you."

Ouch. That hurt.

Eddie held me for only a little while longer before he finally let me go.

"Let's just work on being good parents right now. I'm trying to work and move up in the company. I'm trying to just figure out everything as I go along. You're out of work, so I'm just focused on making sure that the boys are straight. And in order for them to be straight, I have to make sure that you are straight too."

I'm glad that he mentioned money. Eddie turned his back to me but suddenly I got an idea. If he wouldn't give us another chance because I was asking him to, maybe he would consider it with a little incentive.

"Eddie? If you won't give us another chance for love...would you do it for money? Twenty million dollars to be exact."

Eddie turned around to face me.

Well, now that I have his attention…

****

Chapter 3

I explained Patrice's will requirements to Eddie the other day, but I'd added a few things of my own.

I'd told him that not only did we have to be married within a year, I lied and told him that we would receive half of the money and that we had to stay married at least one year after in order to receive the other half. Of course that part was a lie, but if I could convince him to marry me again in the first place, by the time that year was up I would have definitely found a way to get him to love me again.

I also said that there were little things in there such as we had to be faithful to the marriage the entire time and things like that; just to make him a little more comfortable about me, considering my recent whorish ways. I wanted to assure him that I wouldn't step out on him again.

Sure Eddie loved to work and make his own money but let's be honest; who wouldn't want to be a millionaire? But still Eddie hadn't agreed to give us another try or anything. But I was sure that he was thinking about it. And that was a start.

I walked outside just in time to see Polo passing by…again.

Mr. Obsessive turned the corner and headed up the street.

I just wished that he would go away, but I knew that he wouldn't. He was the only thing standing in the way of me and Eddie. If Polo didn't feel anything for me, Eddie would have probably taken me back a long time ago. I was sure of it.

I just had to find a way to get rid of him.

Getting settled into my car, I called Micki.

"Hey Micki."

I hadn't heard much from her since she'd started dating her mysterious white guy. I could only assume that it wasn't all that serious yet since she hadn't introduced him, but he sure had been getting a whole lot of her time because she had been out of sight and out of mind for quite some time.

"I'm never going to get married!"

Uh oh.

"What happened?"

"Girl everything was fine for a while. He even acted like he was falling for me. When I would ask for a commitment he would only say that love is patient and it is kind. But that was a damn lie! Love is blind! And girl he had me seeing all kinds of mess that wasn't true. And guess what, he was still married. He was lying the whole time. His wife called his phone while he was sleeping, in my bed, and I picked it up. She told me everything. Hell and I told her the truth. I told her that I thought her husband loved me. And the bitch laughed in my face. She said to send him home when I was done," Micki said disappointed as I gasped.

"Oh no! And what did you do?"

"Girl, I pretended that I was going to go down on him and I went down alright. I tried to bite the head off of it, and then I did just as his wife instructed me to do. I sent his lying, cheating ass right on home to her."

Good girl.

As if I had room to talk. I'd just kissed Polo not too long ago and secretly I'd wished that he had kissed on something else.

Immediately, I shook away the thought that had just crossed my mind and replaced it with a thought of Eddie.

Eddie.

I love Eddie.

"So, I guess it's back to the drawing board for me. Why did Patrice have to be so damn difficult? She could have just left us with the money for putting up with her obnoxious, spoiled, bitchy self for all of those years. She's dead. It ain't like she can spend the money or something," Micki managed to laugh as I agreed.

But it wouldn't have been Patrice to make things so easy.

"Well, I'm still working on Eddie. Time is moving so fast. Even if I don't get the money, I still want Eddie back. I wouldn't care if I had to go back to work. Hell, I'm bored out of my mind anyway."

I hadn't found a job and to be honest I'd stopped looking. With everything going on, I hadn't even thought about it. Eddie always made sure that the boys and I had plenty since he'd gone back to work. To be honest, I wouldn't be surprised if he gave me his whole check. He was still so good to me; despite what I'd done and despite how hard he tried to hide it with his words and his attitudes. And I couldn't forget that Patrice had set up a publishing company to look at my book. I'd finished it a while ago but I'd wanted to go back over it. I just hadn't found the time or the energy to do it.

"Everything is going to be fine," I said to Micki.

She didn't respond.

"Hello?"

"Sassi?"

"What?"

She took a deep breath.

"There's something that I have to tell you."

"What? What is it?"

Micki started to say something and then the phone went in and out as though someone was calling on the other line.

"I'll call you right back," she said and with that she was gone.

Placing the phone in the passenger side seat, I wondered what it was that she had to tell me. We all knew that Micki couldn't hold water, so there was no telling what kind of beans she was about to spill. But I couldn't wait to find out.

The phone started to ring again, and I reached for it thinking that it was her calling right back. I answered it without looking at it.

"Hello."

"I was thinking that there's no harm in us chatting on the phone. As long as I stay away," Polo said as I looked at the phone and saw that he'd made sure to call private.

"No. I don't want to talk to you Polo."

"Then why do you keep answering the phone?"

"You got a point there," I said and I hung the phone.

I blocked Private Calls and sat the phone down.

But as I drove, I picked it back up and unblocked them.

I cleared my head and drove to the grocery store to get a few more ingredients to go with that night's dinner.

I always made sure to cook when I knew that Eddie would either be coming over to see the boys, or to pick them up or drop them off. I needed for him to miss what it was like being at home.

With me.

With us

Arriving at the store, I headed inside in a hurry.

"Excuse me?"

I looked at the lady as I grabbed a cart.

She was dirty, thin and my guess was that she was homeless. I reached for my purse assuming that she was about to ask for spare change.

"Are you still with Eddie?"

I looked at her confused.

"Excuse me? What did you say? Do I know you?"

She shook her head.

"But you know my husband?" She nodded.

Of course Eddie and I weren't still married, but she didn't need to know that. I waited on her to explain as I tried to reach her a few bucks.

"I don't need your money."

She could've fooled the hell out of me. She was dressed in rags but looking at her face I could see that she was actually really pretty and she had the whitest teeth that I'd ever seen and she smelled good too.

Nope. She was definitely not homeless.

"I'm only dressed like this because I'm a senior in college and this is a part of a study for a paper that I'm writing."

I nodded.

"How do you know Eddie?"

"I don't know him personally. My sister does."

For some reason I got a bad feeling all at once and I started to look around me. Maybe she was going to reveal that her sister was Eddie's new woman or something.

I wasn't sure. But I was listening.

"Maybe I shouldn't say anything."

"Please do. To be honest we are divorced but working on getting back together and by all means if there is something that I need to know please tell me."

She breathed.

"I don't know if I should."

"Don't worry. What's said here will stay between me and you. I promise," I could tell that she was a little timid.

"Well I would hope that our conversation didn't get back to him. Hell if he'll try to set up his own wife, there's no telling what he would try to do to me."

What was she talking about?

Eddie tried to set me up?

How?

When?

"Did some drugs mysteriously end up in your purse one day? A while back?"

"Yes. How did you know that?"

"Your husband, well, ex-husband now, was responsible for that."

What?

I knew exactly what she was referring to.

The time that I'd found the weed in my bag and assumed that Polo had somehow put them there.

"I was in the car with my sister. Eddie paid her to put drugs, a pound of weed in your car one day and then instructed her to tip off the police afterwards. He'd told her that you always leave your car doors unlocked so we'd followed you here, to the grocery store. The only problem was that for whatever reason that day, you actually did lock your car doors. So she had to come up with another plan. We'd watched you go into the store and everything. That's how I recognized you. Stella, my sister, got the idea of trying to see if she could slip some of the drugs in the big purse that you were carrying. I told her that she was crazy, but she'd said that he had already paid her, so she had to figure out how to get it done. She'd said that she didn't have a choice. So she took half of the weed, and went into the store behind you."

"No. Wait a minute. You have to be mistaken."

"I promise you...I'm not."

"So you are telling me, Eddie, my husband at the time, the father of my babies and the man that I was married to for years, tried to do something to get me put in jail?"

Hell no!

I just couldn't believe that it had been Eddie and not Polo that had been behind the drugs in my purse.

"Yes. It was Eddie. A minute or two after going in after you, she came back out and said that she'd done it. I don't know how in the hell she pulled it off but she had. She came out without the weed and said that she'd managed to get it in your purse. She called the police and said that a drug deal was taking place at the store and she had proof. We left just as the first cop and dog arrived. She wasn't sure that they believed her since they'd only sent one cop, but a picture of the cop was the proof that she'd needed to send Eddie to let him know that the job was done."

What!

I couldn't believe my ears.

Eddie had done that to me?

He'd really tried to have me thrown in jail?

As hard as it was for me to believe it, I knew that she was telling the truth.

And I was pissed the hell off!

"How much?"

"What?"

"How much did he pay her? And why would your sister do something like that?"

I wondered if whooping her ass on her sister's behalf was a bit much but somebody had to pay for what could have happened to me.

"$10,000. And she did it for me. I didn't know it at the time. As I said, I'm a senior in college, but I also work full-time and go to school in the evenings. I'd mentioned some tuition trouble, and I was complaining about figuring out how I was going to work overtime to get the money. One day, she came to me and handed me the rest of the money in full. It wasn't the whole ten grand but it was a few thousands. I didn't ask any questions. Since it had been just the two of us since our parents passed away, she always made a way. But then only two days later, we followed you, she told me why she had to go through with it and no matter what I'd said, she'd done her part. Her reasoning was that she'd already spent most the money. The part that she'd given me and the part that she'd kept for herself."

I was so mad that I wanted to cry.

Eddie was so sweet and kind, I just couldn't imagine him doing something like that.

Of all people…Eddie?

He just didn't seem capable of something like this.

"How does she know him?"

"I don't know how my sister knows Eddie. I think that she said that she met him through a friend. Or maybe he was a friend of a guy that she used to date. Something like that. She's years older than me so I'm not sure. Maybe your age or his. But I just thought to say something when I saw you. I always wondered what had happened to you. I didn't know your name but I'd wondered if you'd gotten caught that day and gone to jail or something. But seeing you, I knew that whatever plan that he'd had, probably hadn't worked. I'm glad that it didn't."

She half smiled and started to walk away but she turned back around.

"I don't know the situation, but if I were you, I would get far, far….far away from him. Doesn't seem like the kind of man that I would want to be married to or trying to work things out with," she said and she walked away.

Tell me about it!

Unable to focus, and seeing red, I left the cart where it was and headed back to my car.

Once I was safely inside, I started to scream.

What the hell! You have got to be freaking kidding me!

I screamed, cried and even pressed on the horn a few times.

I know I'd had an affair with his best friend, but damn!

What was he thinking? I could've ended up in jail, or in prison with some kind of felony or something.

Why would he want to do that to me?

He'd tried to have me shipped off to prison or something and he hadn't cared if he'd had to pay to do it.

And $10,000?

Where in the hell had he'd gotten $10,000 when he was having so much financial trouble that I didn't know about? Mentally I'd answered my own question as soon as I'd asked it.

Polo.

Maybe that's why he'd forgiven him so damn fast! He'd needed to borrow some money from him to get rid of me!

I'd heard him say out of his own mouth that he'd wanted to kill me, but I didn't actually think that he'd meant it. I didn't actually think that Eddie had the guts to do something like that. He was harmless. Hell he wouldn't even spank our kids, let alone trying to do something to put me in jail.

So what now?

I continued to bang my hands on the steering wheel in frustration and my soul damn near left my body once someone started to bang on my window.

Polo.

I should have known that he was somewhere lurking!

Without hesitating, and with tears racing down my face, I got out of the car.

"What's wrong? Are you okay?"

"What are you doing here?"

"Uh…"

"Following me again weren't you?"

I was still sobbing and Polo looked concerned.

"What's wrong?"

"You gave the money to Eddie to try to set me up with some kind of drug charges or something?"

Polo looked at me.

"Yes."

What?

I smacked the hell out of him so fast that he didn't even see it coming. I thought that he was going to hit me back or something but he didn't. Instead, he smiled.

"I didn't know what it was for until afterwards."

"Why? Why would he do that to me?"

"He was upset Sassi. He was hurt. He didn't mean it. Hell, I would have done worse."

I bet like hell he would have!

"I didn't know what he needed the money for. I never asked. I never do. But he told me afterwards. That same night. After he saw that you were home and that nothing had happened to you. He was so relieved. He didn't know what he'd been thinking. Trust me. He's sorry. He can't tell you. But I'm telling you for him. He's sorry about that Sassi."

I was just over the whole Eddie and Polo show!

There was just entirely too much that seemed to be going on involving the two of them and after finding out that Eddie had tried to get me in some kind of legal trouble, I was done.

"Bye Polo."

"Wait."

He tried to touch me and I jerked my arm away from him.

"Don't be upset. People do crazy things when they are upset."

"You do crazy things all the time whether you are upset or not," I said sarcastically. He was trying to defend Eddie but I didn't want to hear it.

"Everything that I do I do for a reason or a purpose believe it or not. Eddie didn't mean it Sassi."

"Screw you and your best friend!" I said and I reached for my door handle.

"I still can't keep you off of my mind. No matter how hard I try. I always find myself watching you and wondering about you. Even though I can never have you. I wish there was a way that I could have you Sassi."

Polo half smiled and turned his back to me.

"You can have me now."

Did I just say that?

You damn right I did!

"What?"

"Let's go. To your place. Any place. Right now. I want you to touch me Polo. I want you to make me feel better."

Polo stared at me.

"You're just upset right now Sassi."

"So. I'm upset and I want you to touch me. Will you touch me Polo?" I said to him.

Screw Eddie and his feelings!

Polo just stood there and I continued to plead with him.

"Follow me," he said finally.

I got back into my car and sped out of the parking lot behind him. At that moment all I could feel was hate towards Eddie. Maybe I'd played my part, but who cares!

Who freaking cares!

Polo turned down a side street with me still following behind him. I tried to ignore the voice in my head, but it only grew louder and louder. No matter how mad I was at Eddie, sleeping with Polo was nothing but trouble.

It would only make things worse. And things were already bad enough.

At the changing of the light, Polo went straight and at the last minute, I turned left. Sleeping with him wasn't the answer. It wasn't the solution. I talked to myself aloud, but even I couldn't convince myself not to do more damage than good. Instead of trying to open my legs to Polo, I needed to be trying to find Eddie to give him a piece of my mind! And maybe a two-piece with my fists too!

You know what…

At the stop sign, on the next street, despite my thoughts, I turned around. I turned up the radio to drown out the voice in my head. Glancing briefly into my eyes in the rearview mirror, I frowned but yet I still drove…

All the way to Polo's house.

~***~

"Sassi uh?"

"It's Sassi Sampson…now and forever. How can I help you?"

I was pretty sure that I wasn't going to try to convince Eddie to take me back anymore. Hell, he wouldn't even want me back anyway after all of the nasty, freaky stuff that I'd done to and with Polo the other day.

I just didn't think it was worth it after what I'd found out and I didn't even care if Eddie found out. There was no point in trying to fix something that was obviously broken way before I even had an affair.

But I'd vowed to myself that Polo and I would never cross the line again either. I'd only used him to get back at Eddie, though Eddie didn't even know about it.

"We wanted to know if we could come in and ask you a few questions," the officer said.

I moved out of the way and let them in.

"How can I help you?"

I offered them a seat.

"Well, I know that you're a beneficiary of Patrice Peterson's will correct?"

My stomach started to boil.

Uh oh.

"Yes."

"Well, I'm not sure if you know this but it was changed only two days before she was reported dead."

"Maybe she had a change of heart or something. I didn't know that it was a crime to change your will. I thought that you could change it anytime that you wanted to."

"That's right. And Patrice died from a tumor?"

"Yes. From my understanding. I didn't even know she'd died until afterwards."

"Did you know that there's no record of Patrice going to the hospital within six months of her death? Or to her primary doctor's office?"

What? That just couldn't be true.

I looked at the officer and awaited his next words.

"Are you aware of who Patrice's father is?"

"Of course. We'd been friends for years. He is a big time movie producer but more than anything he was a father."

Once Patrice's mother passed away, he spent all of his time spoiling Patrice, and giving her the world, until he got remarried. He married some French woman, and though he didn't have as much time to spend with Patrice, he loved her like crazy.

"He suspects foul play. He'd finally gotten around to cleaning out her house. He saw a few papers that were supposedly from a doctor about a tumor but he found out that all of the documentation was false. Patrice didn't have a tumor. There were no real records of it. At all."

What!

"Who made the documents, we aren't sure. The doctor on the papers and the prescription bottles is a fake. The doctor doesn't exist. The pills in the bottles were tested and they were just sleeping pills and aspirins. No recent hospital visits. No recent doctor office visits. Her insurance hadn't been used, or billed, for any reason for months. Being that there was so much documentation on the supposedly tumor, her father hadn't demanded an autopsy before. Devastated that his daughter hadn't shared her secret with him, he'd simply grieved and laid her to rest without too many questions. But as he was cleaning out her place, something told him to look a little deeper, and the truth was something that he hadn't expected. The tumor story was a lie. So, now he wants the truth. He wants his daughter exhumed and he wants to know the real reason and cause of her death. He thinks that she was murdered."

I couldn't believe my ears.

So, Patrice didn't die from a tumor?

She was murdered?

Possibly?

Probably?

"And it's from our understanding, from other interviews, that you and Patrice were very close."

"Yes we were. But a lot of people didn't know that we weren't exactly speaking. Actually, I didn't even know that she was in town until after she died."

"But yet you didn't come to the funeral."

"Like I said, I didn't know that she was dead. I didn't find out until after meeting for the will at the lawyers office."

"Um huh. And you two weren't on speaking terms?"

"We weren't. I'd found out that she'd had a sexual relationship with my husband before we were married and with my father. But I didn't do anything to her. I loved her. I wish that I could see her, just on last time."

"Yeah. Everyone says that you two were very close. We don't believe that you had anything to do with her death, but we are sure that someone did. Anyway, we just wanted to make you aware of the matter at hand and I wanted to see if you've heard anything or seen anything suspicious?"

I shook my head no.

"Okay. Well, if you do, could you please let me know? In the meantime, we will be digging up Patrice's body to see what the real reason behind her death was. I got a feeling that we will be dealing with a homicide. But let's hope that I'm wrong," the officer gave me his card and headed out the door.

I took a deep breath and stared at the officer's card in my hand.

What the hell was going on around here?

I took a seat.

Patrice didn't have a tumor?

But she was dead.

So the question was…who in the hell killed Patrice?

And why?

~***~

I stared at Eddie.

I wanted to stab him or punch him in the face or something.

"What's your problem?"

His phone started to ring and he glanced at it.

But he didn't pick it up.

"Who is that?"

"None of your business Sassi."

With what the cops had told me about Patrice, my mind had been all messed up lately. I couldn't help but wonder who would have wanted to kill her. And furthermore, I wondered if I knew her killer.

Patrice was a difficult woman, so it could have been a number of folks that probably wanted nothing more than to see her dead. But my intuition was telling me that somebody around me knew something.

And somebody was going to slip up at sooner or later, so my eyes were open.

Hell, I wondered about Eddie. If he would have drugs put in my bag to try to have me sent to jail, was he capable of murder too? And what would have been his motive? We were past the confession of his and Patrice's past relationship, so he wouldn't have had any reason to want her dead.

But somebody did.

Of course I hadn't heard anything else from the cops about it or anything, but only time would tell.

Eddie's phone made another noise and he picked it up.

He smiled but hurriedly made it disappear.

"What?"

"Nothing."

"What are you doing?"

"Nothing."

He put his phone back down.

"Who is that on your phone Eddie huh? Obviously they are making you smile."

"I don't know what you're talking about Sassi."

Eddie started to play with our youngest son and simply ignored me and my questions, turned his phone on silent and put it in his pocket.

For the rest of the evening we barely said a few words to each and once he was gone, I sat in front of my laptop and got to work. Our phones were still on the same plan since he paid the bill. So, let's see what I could find out.

I created an online account with our cell phone carrier. The phones were in Eddie's name, but of course I knew all of his information so it really didn't make a difference.

I started to look around. Immediately I noticed something wrong. Imagine my surprise to see that it wasn't just two lines on our account...there were three.

Who in the hell has the third line?

Immediately I grabbed my phone and dialed the number. I called private a few times, back to back, but no one answered the phone.

Hmm...

Why in the hell had he never mentioned this before?

Sure even when I worked, I had some bills that I took care of but Eddie had always been very proactive, busy, but very much so in the loop, especially when finances and bills were involved.

The cell phone just happened to be one of the bills that he'd always handled.

And now I know why.

I went looking through everything else. I came across the monthly bills and guess what else they had...statements!

I couldn't see text messages, but I could see each lines total usage and call logs.

The mystery line didn't have one single outgoing call to Eddie, not even once.

But the other line was very active. It had called other numbers before so I called a few of the numbers that were listed.

A few folks answered the private calls but none of the voices belonged to anyone that I recognized. I always stayed on the phone until they hung up.

Just in case they uttered a name but they never did.

I headed to study Eddie's calls more in depth.

There were plenty of calls back and forth from mine, his parents, and even Polo. There were even a few from my mother but there were a good bit from another mysterious number.

Maybe this was the number of whoever had been making him smile. They talked often. There were at these twenty calls either made or answered from the number so I dialed that number too. This had to be some woman that he was seeing but I was about to mess it all the way up.

I waited to see if someone to answer and finally they did.

"Hello?" she said.

At first I just sat there.

I didn't say anything as she repeated hello a few more times. Finally, I figured that I might as well at least ask her name. And I could think of a few more questions that I wanted to ask her too.

"Who is this?" I asked.

"You called me remember? So, who is this?" she asked politely.

"I'm Eddie's wife," I said to her.

"Oh really? Is that so? Funny. I thought that I was."

What the hell!

****

Chapter 4

"How the hell did you get in my house Polo?"

It was 3 a.m. in the morning and I woke up to find Polo sitting on the edge of the bed looking at me.

"I stole Eddie's key and made a copy of it."

"If you don't get your crazy ass out of here I'm calling the police!" I bellowed.

"I'm not crazy. I knew that I might need it one day."

Polo was a lunatic!

"I love you Sassi."

"Get out Polo!"

"I need to talk to you about something."

"At three in the morning? And you couldn't call me private like you always do to talk to me about it?"

I pulled the cover up around my neck to make sure that none of my naked frame was exposed. It wasn't like he hadn't seen all of my good stuff but I had enough on my plate already and I didn't need to keep bringing Polo into the mix. Again.

So, of course the woman, on the phone, from the other night was only kidding about being Eddie's wife. She and Eddie weren't married. She was just being a bitch because I'd called her phone.

But she did reveal to me that she and Eddie had been getting to know each other for a little while, which he'd conveniently never mentioned.

She even knew the truth about what had happened with us and that I was the one that had stepped out on our marriage and cheated with his best friend. As private as Eddie was, I was surprised that he'd told some woman so much. I couldn't believe that he'd told her what I'd done to him, which could only mean one thing. He liked her and he was really trying to move forward with her.

But for some reason, I didn't really care as much as I thought that I would and of course the drug incident had something to do with that I was sure.

He'd even let her meet our kids, so the truth to the matter was that bastard had no plans on giving us another chance, and considering what I'd found out at the grocery store, he didn't have to.

I stared at Polo.

Nah. We could never be anything more.

I wasn't Eddie's biggest fan at the moment but I had to stop entertaining things with Polo too. As we all know, if you keep playing with fire, you are bound to get burned. And I'd set fire to enough things in my life already.

"I've convinced Eddie to take you back."

I looked at him confused. One minute he says he loves me.

The next minutes he's trying to hook me back up with his best friend, who I didn't even want anymore.

"No thanks, I'll pass."

"Don't say that. You both still love each other."

"It's too late. I don't think that I want him back. And besides, he's moved on. But I'm sure that you know that already."

"Who? Lola? Oh no. He was hoping that you found out just to make you jealous. She's a nice girl, but his heart belongs to you."

Well, of course Polo would know the truth if anyone did, but knowing him, his proposition came with a catch and I didn't have time to play around with Polo, Eddie, or even my life anymore.

I just wanted to be happy.

"I'm worried about him. Eddie isn't as put together as you may think Sassi."

"What do you mean Polo?"

"I'm not the only one pretty good at pretending. He needs you. He's miserable and I can see it. As his best friend, as his brother, I have to try to fix this. I have to make it right."

"Polo, it's just too late."

"No it isn't. I'm going to disappear for a while. I told Eddie that I was going to go on a long vacation, to get myself together. I'll be back. But by then, you and Eddie should be fine; maybe even headed back down the road towards marriage or something. I'm doing this because I love him. I'm doing this because I love you."

For the first time, like ever, Polo seemed to become emotional. And I couldn't believe the words that were coming out of his mouth.

He was so crazy, and unstable, that you never knew how to take him. But as I always said. If he didn't love anybody, he loved Eddie. That was the only thing that I knew for sure.

"I don't know if that's possible after…"

"Sassi you didn't even go to jail," Polo said knowing that I was about to mention the drugs that Eddie had some woman to put in my purse.

"Polo that's not the point."

"Then what is? You didn't get hurt. Nothing came from what he'd tried to do. He wasn't thinking straight. He was in a bad space. Forgive him and move on. If he forgives you for what you did with me, you surely can forgive him."

I guess he had a point.

"Forgive him Sassi. You're fine. Nothing happened to you. I've had this same talk with him too. I told him that he needed to forgive you and fix things with you. To be honest, I think that he just wanted my blessing. He's going to completely try to forgive you and work things out. He trusts my judgement. He trusts my opinion. I screwed him over but I think he just wanted to know that if he continued to love you that I wouldn't be an issue anymore. I won't. So get over it. I know him ten times better than you do Sassi and he needs this. He needs you. Patch things up. I won't stay gone forever. But I'll stay gone long enough.

With me out of the way, you two will fall head over heels in love again. I'm sure of it."

This was so grown-up of Polo that it was almost a turn on.

I admired his selflessness. This isn't what I expected from him and it made him look so damn sexy in a sense.

I sat up.

I thought about the past and the future. I thought about what I'd done with Polo and even about the woman that Eddie was dating. I thought about forever.

"We have a third phone on our phone bill. Do you know who it belongs to?"

"No," Polo said bluntly.

Well, he was probably lying, but I guess that was something that I could ask Eddie.

"I'm giving you what I know that you want. I'm going away. I'm going to leave in the morning."

I stared at Polo.

I couldn't believe that he was doing this for us. Maybe he just really did care about Eddie's happiness.

I took a deep breath.

I thought about my life and what I wanted for myself and my kids. I thought about my future.

Maybe Eddie and I could try this thing again. I guess I could get over what he'd done to me and just move forward. If he could get over my wrongs, I could surely get over his.

"Okay."

Polo nodded.

He still appeared extremely sad and a part of me wanted to comfort him. He really didn't have anybody, but Eddie, that didn't just want to use him, so the fact that he was willing to go off for a while, all alone, I knew that he really had to be concerned about Eddie and his happiness.

"Thank you. Though I'm a little made at him, I do still love him you know."

"I know," Polo said and stood to his feet.

Polo was wearing gym shorts and a tee-shirt.

He had his hair in a pony-tail and even though he wasn't trying to be sexy or attractive, he absolutely was!

"I'm doing this for him Sassi. And whether you believe me or not, in my own way, I really do care about you."

I believed him.

"One time for the road," Polo grinned

"Get your ass out of here," I said to him.

He couldn't help but chuckle.

"Bye Sassi. I love you," Polo said as he turned and walked away.

I love you too, my heart said, but my mouth remained silent as I pressed my lips together.

Well, here goes nothing!

The next morning, the smell of bacon woke me up.

I headed downstairs to find Eddie cooking breakfast with the boys.

"Good morning."

I smiled and kissed the boys.

Eddie got the boys together, fixed us both a plate and carried them to the living room as I followed him. I was sure that it wouldn't be a good idea to mention that Polo had come by last night, but there was something that I had to get off of my chest.

"Who is the third line on our phone account for?"

Eddie looked at me before sipping his orange juice.

"What are you talking about?"

"There's a third line on our phone plan. Who does it belong to? Who has that phone?"

"I don't know what you're talking about Sassi."

That was always his answer these days but I was about to show him. I headed to grab my laptop and I sat close beside him so that he could see. I logged into our phone account and headed to the section to show him what I was talking about.

What? Where is it?

The account was now only showing two lines: Eddie's and mine.

But I was sure that it had been a third line there. I tried to search for it in past months and on previous statements just as I had only a few nights ago, but nothing was there.

What? I know what I saw.

"Wait a minute," I said to Eddie and headed upstairs to get my phone.

I found the number that belonged to the other phone line and I called it. See, I knew that it had been there.

"The number you are trying to reach is invalid. Please check the number and try your call again. Message VZTV3."

What the hell?

What was going on around here?

I know damn well that I hadn't been dreaming that time and I didn't understand why the number was now invalid and why it had completely vanished from Eddie's account.

I headed back downstairs.

"What were you saying?" Eddie asked.

I sat across from him and picked up my breakfast.

"Nothing. Nothing at all," I said.

Either my mind was playing tricks on me or somebody was trying to make me think that I was crazy.

And I had a feeling that somebody was Eddie.

~***~

Time was flying by and for the most part, things were okay.

I tried to sit all of my feelings aside and thing about the big picture, and with that being said, Eddie and I were dating...literally.

We were taking things slow and actually dating each other again. And actually, honestly, I was kind of enjoying it. It seemed as though this time I was learning the real him and now that I was older and after all that we'd been through, the real him wasn't all that bad. The real him was good enough for me. We seemed to get along better than ever and we seemed to be a lot more open with each other, though there were a few things that I was still keeping from him.

I never mentioned to Eddie that I'd found out that he was responsible for having the drugs put in my purse. I hadn't mentioned it to him at all. Polo told me that he hadn't told him that I knew, so it was nothing more than a thing of the past.

It was forgiven. Just like he had forgiven me.

Speaking of Polo, he was gone. He had been gone for the past two months. From checking Eddie's phone, he barely even called him. Maybe once a week, if that, so I figured that he felt that staying away really was for the best.

Eddie never spoke about him to me and I was sure that even if we did work things out, things would never be the same. I'd ruined everything that we had over sex but what I discovered was that sex wasn't everything.

And sex will never be better than real, genuine love.

Sex was good. Real good between Polo and I. But at the end of the day, I needed more than a good nut every day.

Right now, I just needed love.

The kids and Eddie had gone to take care of a few errands so I figured that I would head out to go do a few things for myself.

"Whoa," the officer said.

He was about to knock.

"Hi."

"Hi. Were you on your way out?"

"I was but I wasn't going anywhere important."

It had been a long while since I'd heard anything from the police about Patrice and the possibly murder case. Last I'd heard they were running tests on her to see if they could find a cause of death. She'd been gone for a while now, so they didn't know if they would have any luck, but they'd wanted to try.

I was more than curious about the outcome because if Patrice had been murdered than that meant that they were going to be on the hunt for her killer. And I wouldn't get a wink of sleep until they found out who it was.

"Well, we didn't have any luck determining the cause of death. The things that they could test they did. But it wasn't enough left of her to discover much. So much had been removed to get her ready for burial you know. And with time going by, it just made things a little more difficult. Especially not knowing what we were looking for. No strange prints or anything were found at her house. No forced entry. Nothing that would be enough to rule it as a homicide. I just stopped by to let you know."

I took a deep breath.

I hated the fact that her father would never have the closure that he was looking for and that Patrice might have had her life taken from her a little too soon.

I mean, sure, she was a bitch; all day. Every day.

But she didn't deserve to die and especially to be killed.

And now we wouldn't never know what really happened to her.

"The only thing that we could be sure of was that there was no diagnosis or records of her having a tumor, so we can assure you that wasn't the cause of death. Other than that, we will never know much else.

"Thank you for letting me know."

The officer nodded and walked away. Just as he drove away, Micki pulled up and parked beside of me.

"What's wrong?"

I hadn't seen her in a little while since Eddie and I had been spending all of our time together. In a way she looked different. She seemed to be glowing or something.

"He was just filling me in on Patrice. They said that more than like she was murdered.

"Oh yeah. They told me that too," she said.

"Didn't you go to the doctors with her a few times? And what about her not wanting to stay at the hospital right before she died? The day that you took Mama there for her to apologize to her? They said that there was no hospital records for her. How is that possible?"

"Yes. All I know is what she told me. I did go to the doctor office with her, once or twice, but I always sat in the car. She'd said that she needed me to drive her when it was over, and she would go in and an hour or so later, she would come out. If they have no records, just as I told them, I don't understand. I know for a fact that she went to the doctor's office."

Hmm…

Then why wouldn't they have any record of her visit?

"And even when going to the hospital, before she died, she was already there. She was outside in her car when I got there and said that she refused to stay. That's when she asked me to call your mother so that she could apologize. All her papers and medicine was for a tumor."

Hmmm…

"It was all fake. The papers. The medicine. The doctors that prescribed it. It was all fake. Patrice more than likely did not die from any kind of tumor. They said there were no hospital or doctor visits from her, for months."

I really wondered what it was that Patrice had been involved in. Maybe she was planning to fake her death and something happened before she could go through with her plan.

Why she would want to do it?

I didn't know. I was just coming up with possibilities since things just didn't make sense.

"Well, I don't know Sassi. I really don't know."

And neither did I.

"Well not to change the subject but…I'm getting married. And I was hoping that you would be my maid of honor."

Hearing her break the news automatically made me think about Patrice's will. I hadn't thought about it much lately but time was ticking and I wasn't sure if Eddie and I were going to make the deadline.

"Really? Congratulations. To who?"

"Your brother," Micki said.

Really?

Of course my brother was the father of one of Micki's kids but I was surprised. They hated each other. He was the definition of a dead beat daddy, and for years Micki gave him hell about taking care of his responsibilities and then finally she just gave up.

But they were getting married? It had to be for the money.

And why was I the last to know?

"For love or money?"

"Is doing it for both such a bad thing?"

"Nope. Not at all my sista'. Not at all," I said.

We chatted for a little while longer and then we headed in separate directions.

I was supposed to go get my hair done, but I decided to go do a little shopping instead. I could barely fit any of my clothes. I seemed to be getting bigger, but I was barely eating so I was mad that my body was doing the opposite of what I'd hoped it would do. Humph, but I was still sexy.

The gentleman held the door for me as I entered the store.

"Thank you," I smiled.

"No problem."

He went one way, and I went in another direction.

I kept looking up and catching him looking up at me.

Finally, he walked over to me.

"I just couldn't help but notice how beautiful you are," he said.

"Thanks. And I can't help but notice that you're in a ladies department store. So, that must mean that you have a wife, or a girlfriend," I said to him.

"Or a teenaged daughter," he nodded at the young girl a few racks from us. She waved in smiled.

"Oops. Sorry," I laughed.

"No problem. So, I don't see a ring on your finger. Does that mean that you're single? I sure hope so."

He was coming on to me.

Was it bad that I was just a little bit flattered?

"Well, my ex-husband and I are giving it a try, one more time, so, I guess that means that I'm somewhat taken," I answered.

"Man. That's too bad. I mean. Not bad that you are trying it again. I've been there, done that. Just too bad that you're not available," he said with a smile.

And what an amazing smile it was. His pearly white teeth made me want to lick him.

"Is it too serious to where you wouldn't consider giving me your number?"

"Yeah. I believe it is."

"Well, in another lifetime, be on the lookout for me. Because I'll definitely keep an eye out for you," he said.

"Likewise," and just as he turned around, the sound of a gun went off.

Everyone screamed but me.

I was in shock, and I couldn't seem to force my feet to move. I looked up to see that it was Carmen, the woman with the HIV, holding the gun.

"Hey Sassi with an "I". I just saved your life girlie. You're welcome," she said and she walked out of the store as though she hadn't done a thing.

The next hour or so, I was questioned and had to give statement after statement.

"How did you know the deceased?"

"I didn't. He approached me in the store."

"How did you know the suspect?"

"I don't know her. I met her once at the hospital. She'd said that she'd just saved my life."

"Meaning?"

"Meaning he was probably trying to charm her out of her panties so that he could give her a share of his disease too. Lucky for you. You didn't get to join the club," a woman said behind me.

"Hi. I'm his wife," she said to the police and they told me that it was okay for me to leave.

I committed about fifty traffic violations, trying to get home. Carmen had killed the man that had made her sick. I wondered where she'd come from and whether or not she'd been watching him or intended to kill him. She must have thought that I was going to fall for him or something.

I told you.

That woman was my guardian angel or something. Though I was pretty sure angels weren't killing anyone. Still in shock that I'd seen someone killed right in front of me, I smiled at the sight of Eddie and the boys and I ran into his arms.

"What? What is it?"

"Nothing."

This world and the people in it were crazy and I was lucky to have a man that loved me enough to want me and only me. And never, ever, would I take the love that Eddie had for me for granted again.

Ever!

~***~

The music was heavenly.

I was smiling so hard that my cheeks hurt. I was looking ahead but I didn't really see anyone. All I could see was the back of him. He was waiting for me. He was waiting to make me his wife. Today was the happiest day of my life and this time I was happy. I was genuinely happy. The music stopped and finally I reached the altar as he reached for my hand. He looked at me with love and his eyes and all I managed to see was forever.

Forever with my king. Forever with my love.

Forever with...

Polo.

I opened my eyes.

Yikes!

Thank goodness that was only a dream. I looked next to me to see that Eddie was sleeping beside of me. Just the way that I liked it. Just the way that it was supposed to be.

I tapped him, and he turned over.

"Were you asleep?"

"No. I was just laying here think of how bad I want to make love to you," Eddie said.

I was surprised to hear him say it since he was the one that insisted on us taking things turtle-slow. He wouldn't even stay over every night and most of the time when he did, he slept with the boys. He'd only slept in bed with me this time because we had been watching a movie, and both fell asleep.

Though he tried to act like he had, I wasn't sure that he had completely forgiven me just yet. He was trying to but there were some days where he looked at me like he just wanted to punch me in the face. Especially on nights that he would be leaving to go home to his parents and the boys would ask him why he couldn't stay. He always gave me that look as if to say that I'd ruined our lives. I had. But we were working on it.

I never even told him about the man at the store and the woman Carmen who had shot him. I'd watched the news to see if they ever caught her, but they were saying it was as though she'd just vanished. Either way, I was thankful for the words that she'd given me and I was trying my best to apply them to my situation with Eddie. And from the looks of it, I was making some progress.

"Well, if I give you some of this, just so you know, we go together," I laughed.

Surprisingly, Eddie did too.

"I'm okay with that," he said and he kissed me.

He kissed me hard, forcefully. To be honest, he kissed me like Polo. It almost creeped me out but after a while, I started to enjoy it.

"I love you Eddie. I really do."

"Do you really?"

"More than anything in the world."

"Prove it," was all that he said and I stood up to remove my sleep wear.

Briefly I wondered if he was going to be able to hang. I was almost nervous because I didn't want anything to change my mind about wanting us to work.

"Lay on your back," Eddie instructed me.

He was about to put that golden tongue of his on me and my insides got all excited and stuff. If I didn't miss anything else, sexually, I definitely missed that and it didn't take long for Eddie to remind me.

In just a matter of seconds, my eyes started to flutter and wished that I could cut his tongue off and keep it in my back pocket, to use whenever I wanted to.

"Tell me you love me," Eddie said in between licks and I told him that I loved him over and over again.

My body started to heat up, but for the first time ever, I didn't want to come from his mouth. I wanted to see if his wood could do the job.

"Make love to me Eddie," I said, giving him a hint that I wanted to feel him inside of me.

Eddie entered me and I looked him in the eyes.

"I love you," he said and I bit my bottom lip.

Stop talking and show me what you got!

And boy did he show me. It wasn't the best sex that we'd ever had, but it was good. And I do mean real good.

Eddie and I cuddled, out of breath and we both managed to fall back asleep.

I was happy. I was satisfied.

Then why was I now dreaming about Polo...again?

~***~

"Hello?"

"It's me."

The number was private but I automatically I knew who it was.

Polo.

Honestly, that's the reason I'd answered it. At this point it was almost four months, and he hadn't been seen and barely heard from.

Eddie was washing my car, so I got up and made my way inside. I stood in the window so that I could see him ahead of time whenever he decided to come in.

"How is he?"

"Why didn't you just call and ask him yourself?"

"I do call. But we don't talk about his emotions."

"He's fine. We're fine."

I guess I could ask about him. Nothing was wrong with asking about him.

"And how are you Polo?"

"Well, I miss home. I miss Eddie. And I miss you."

"You don't miss me."

"Yes, I do. But I know this was the right thing to do. I don't want to come back until you guys are headed back down the aisle, again, or standing in the courthouse, smiling from ear to ear. I owe him happiness. I owe him everything. He's done a lot for me for years. But well, you know."

Yes. I did. I've always hated how Eddie ran to Polo's rescue but no matter what time of day it was, no matter where Polo was at, if Polo was in trouble, Eddie went running.

It had been that way our entire marriage. It would have probably been that way for the rest of our lives; had I not messed up their friendship or at least shaken it up a bit.

"Where are you?"

"Far, far away from having to watch you guys fall in love again."

He sounded sad, but I tried to force myself not to care.

"Well, I just wanted to hear your voice. I have plenty of videos of you with me, so I get to see you, and your booty, every day."

Okay. Here's the real Polo.

"So you really did have copies of the footages that I deleted?"

"Of course. I've been into technology, cameras, and things like that since I was very young. I guess that was something else that I was good at other than my sex and my sex toys. I always make copies. Of everything. You never know when you may need it or when it may come in handy. In this case, watching you on my recordings is enough to keep me from trying to come back to see you physically. Since we will never be, my confession is that I used to see you every day; whether you knew it or not. I've seen you every day since the first time I saw you all those years ago. Well, unless I'm out of town or something, but you get my point."

"Yeah, you're a damn stalker."

"No. I just admire and crave to look at beautiful things. You've always been beautiful to me."

His words and his charm were dangerous! That's what had gotten me in trouble the first time!

"Okay Polo, well nice talking to you I guess," I said to him.

"Bye Sassi. I'll see you whenever you guys tie the knot. Whenever that will be."

With that he hung up. I put the phone in my pocket and stared out the window at Eddie. I watched him with a smile but my mind was all over the place.

Was this really what I wanted?

Did I really want forever with Eddie?

I entertained thoughts of Eddie years and years from now, and also I envisioned what forever with Polo might look like.

After a few minutes, finally I shook my head.

The obvious choice was Eddie.

But why did my heart seem to want to choose Polo instead?

****

Chapter 5

I only had a month left before it would be time to meet back up with Patrice's lawyer.

Micki and my brother were set to get married in two weeks, but Eddie and I didn't seem to be any closer than we were months ago. But I couldn't blame him, nor could I complain.

Things were between us were great. We were laughing again and having decent sex, regularly. I wasn't sure if he was sneaking and taking the pills or not, but so far, he hadn't had a two-minute episode.

Yes!

Maybe it really was just stress from him trying to keep his company and all of the financial issues that he was hiding from me at the time in order. But so far, so good.

I no longer felt confused, or torn in between the two. Eddie was what was best for me. He was going to love me and take care of me, and now that my mind and heart were on one accord, I just wanted forever with my Eddie.

"Let's go to church."

It was a Sunday morning and Eddie had stayed over.

"Church?"

I couldn't remember the last time that we'd gone to church together. It had been years. But maybe church was just what we needed.

"Okay."

After another hour or so, we were all dressed and headed out the door.

"Sassi, I'm not a perfect man. I've made mistakes."

I looked at Eddie.

"We all have. But at some point you have to just forgive and forget those mistakes and move forward. Leave all the mistakes in the past and just look towards the future," I said to him and he nodded.

"Yeah. The future."

We pulled up at Eddie's parent's church.

They still weren't too excited about Eddie and I being so close these days, but I didn't care what they thought about me. As long as Eddie could forgive and love me, that was all that mattered. And his father was no saint himself.

Maybe he needed a reminder of his transgressions with Polo's mother, before he whispered anything in Eddie's ear about mine.

We walked into the church and it seemed as though all eyes were on us. They were. But mine were on everything else. Instead of there being a service, there were people, Eddie's family and even some of mine, standing there.

There were decorations, flowers at the front of the altar and Eddie's pastor was standing there.

Mama was there. And Micki and my brother were there too.

I hadn't even noticed any of their cars in the parking lot.

My mother motioned for my boys to come to her and Eddie grabbed my hand and led me to the altar.

"We have been through a lot, but I know that I can't live without you. This has nothing to do with the money or Patrice's will. This has nothing to do with the past and the mistakes. This has to do with you and me. Even if we never see a dime of those millions, I want to give us another shot. Another shot at love. Another shot at the future and at happiness. But this time we have to do this right."

I wanted to cry but I didn't.

Yes! Yes!

This time I wouldn't mess this up. This time no one and nothing would come in between us. Eddie pulled out a ring box from his pocket. It seemed as though he gave me all of his money, but apparently he had been keeping some of it to get me a new ring.

"Before the Man above, the pastor and all of our family, I want to ask for your forgiveness. For things I have done; known and unknown. For things I've thought about doing that I knew weren't right. I'm asking you to forgive me."

"Of course. And forgive me for what I did Eddie. I'm so sorry. It will never happen again."

Eddie smiled.

"I forgive you," he said. "And am I the husband for you? Do you believe in your mind and with all of your heart that we can make it to the end this time? That we have what it takes? If you don't you can say it. Right here and right now. No love lost. No hurt feelings."

"Yes Eddie. I love you so much. I want us. I want you. I want forever with you.

"Well, then, right here and right now, will you marry me Sassi, again?"

I smiled at him and nodded as he placed the ring on my finger. He stood up and hugged me.

Mama walked over to me and handed me a bouquet of flowers as I smiled and as tears of joy streamed down my face.

"Pastor before you do anything, pray for us. Please." Eddie said.

And what started off with prayers ended with vows and promises to love through thick and thin and from better and for worse, again. And this time, I'd meant ever word that I'd said.

This time, I was never letting go.

~***~

I stared at her in her wedding gown.

Micki looked absolutely beautiful. And the small veil that slightly covered her face was perfect.

"You look good maid of honor," she said.

"And you don't look half bad yourself bride," I complimented her.

"I wish Patrice was here."

"Me too."

The preacher stuck his head in and told us that it was time to get this show on the road.

And for the next hour, everything was like a fairytale. The wedding was beautiful to say the least. I couldn't help but wonder where they had gotten the money from to pay for everything. I guess Micki probably spent all that she had considering that she knew what she would be getting in return. As of that date, we were both married, and that meant that we were both going to be rich. I didn't think I would see the day that my brother settled down and I surely didn't think that it would be with Micki. But hey, she'd been like a sister to me for years.

Now, it was on paper.

Micki approached me at the reception with a smile.

"Girl, I'm married now chile," she chimed.

I wiggled my finger at her.

"Welcome darling. Welcome."

I smiled at her but she looked as though she was going to cry. Her happy, glowing smile was gone.

"What? What's wrong?"

She looked at me.

"What Micki?"

She took a deep breath. She opened her mouth but then she closed it.

"Spit it out."

"Remember when I told you that I had something to tell you?"

I'd forgotten all about that. For some reason my heart sank into the pit of my belly.

What was it?

Micki opened her mouth to speak but my brother, her husband, interrupted us and started pulling Micki towards the dance floor. She mouthed something to me but I couldn't make out what it was. I had a bad feeling that whatever she was going to reveal had something to do with Patrice. And I was willing to bet my life on it that I wasn't going to like it.

What did she have to tell me?

~***~

"Polo is coming home tomorrow," Eddie said.

I looked at him. I was surprised that he'd even mentioned Polo's name to me. I knew that he would be back sooner or later, but for some reason I felt nervous.

"Okay. So, we all know that you guys are going to remain friends. Of course our relationship as a whole will never be the same so what does that mean?"

Of course Eddie had moved into the apartment with me and the kids. But I was also sure that he probably would never trust me and Polo under the same roof or in the same room again.

"Things will never be the same. He will more than likely never come to the house so that means that often me and the kids will probably go to his."

I couldn't argue with that. It was what it was.

"I don't know if that will change as the years go by. I've forgiven you both, but that doesn't mean that I don't think about what both of you did to me from time to time because I do."

"It's fine Eddie. I completely understand."

Eddie smiled and reached me a glass.

"Here, I made you a smoothie."

Eddie always made the best smoothies, ever, so though I was in a rush, I paused for a second.

"I definitely missed waking up to these," I smiled at him.

"Um, and I missed waking up to these," Eddie said squeezing me boobs.

"Stop it."

"Only because you have somewhere to go. When you get back, I plan on putting them into my mouth," Eddie said.

I was definitely enjoying this nasty side of him! The night after we got married again, he gave me the business so good that he left me shaking and begging him for more. Whatever had changed with him, was just what we needed and I knew that now we were going to have the perfect marriage. The one that we'd always deserved.

I placed on my left shoe. I was headed to meet Micki at the lawyer's office. Today was the day that both of us would become millionaires; literally.

I'd told Eddie not to go to work that day and I was going to tell him once the check was in my hand that he never had to go back again.

What was mine was his, and whether he wanted to start a new business or if he just wanted to live for a while, we would have more than enough money to do whatever we wanted to do.

But what I really couldn't wait for was to be face to face with Micki again so that she could tell me what she was about to tell me at her wedding. We hadn't talked much since then, but I was more than ready to talk to her today.

Leaving out, I thought about my life as I drove in silence.

The past two years have been rocky and a never-ending rollercoaster ride, but I was glad that things were going back to normal.

I lost my husband. I got him back.

I lost my dignity and so much more, but everything was back on track. Words couldn't express how thankful I was for second chances.

I pulled up to see that Micki was already there, but she was inside. I grabbed my paperwork proving that Eddie and I were married and I headed inside too.

In less than thirty minutes, we were both walking out with checks in our hands. We stopped by my car and stood quietly in shock for a while.

Did Patrice really leave me twenty million dollars?

What in the hell was I supposed to do with twenty million dollars?

"Micki? Do you feel bad a little knowing that she could have been murdered?" I asked her now feeling some kind now that I had the money in my hand.

"No."

"Do you ever wonder what really happened to her?"

Micki looked at me.

"No."

"Really?"

"If I told you, I would have to kill you."

I looked at her and cracked a smile thinking that she was joking, but she didn't smile at all.

"What?"

"Leave it alone Sassi."

Micki walked away from me and headed to her car.

She opened her car door and looked at me.

"Goodbye Sassi."

What? What did she mean goodbye?

"Goodbye? What are you talking about girl?"

Micki looked at me just before getting into her car.

She started to pull off but she noticed that I was still standing there, so she reversed.

"Oh, by the way, what I was going to tell you was…"

I held my breath and then gasped once she finished her sentence.

"It wasn't a dream."

Micki giggled and sped off.

What?

Wait a minute…

What wasn't a dream?

Huh?

Was she talking about the incident involving the three of them and the mysterious Vanessa woman?

I grabbed my phone but just as I did, I saw that she tossed something out her car window just before turning out of the parking lot. I called her and her phone started to ring against the pavement.

Her last words played in my head over and over again as I got into my car and ran over her phone.

Damn it!

Why did I just do that?

There could have been something in it that I needed to see.

Glancing at it in my rearview mirror, there was no hope for it so I continued to drive but I wasn't going home.

It wasn't a dream?

So I was right?

The incident that had gone on with Eddie, Polo and Micki wasn't a dream?

Then who in the hell is Vanessa?

And how in the hell did they pull it all off?

I was confused.

If it wasn't a dream then how come the pregnancy test was never opened?

Sure I was pregnant, but did that mean that one of them had done something to me to cause me to lose the baby?

And so that meant that Eddie had been lying to me the whole time?

About everything?

And of course that meant that Polo had been lying too.

What the hell!

I pulled up at Micki's house to see that no one was there.

I parked. I wasn't leaving until I got some answers.

I saw that Eddie was calling me but I would deal with him after I dealt with Micki.

How did she know about this Vanessa woman?

Who was she?

What had they done to me?

Why was it such a big secret?

I had so many questions and I wasn't leaving until I got some answers. I called my brother's phone but he didn't answer.

After sitting for another hour or so, and because Eddie was blowing up my phone, finally I decided to leave.

And just as I started to pull off, Polo pulled up beside of me.

He's back.

"What are you doing Sassi?"

"Waiting for Micki to come home."

Polo looked at me as if he was happy to see me.

He was smiling and it was something weird in his eyes.

To be honest, he was giving me the creeps.

"She's not coming home Sassi."

"What do you mean?

"I saw her at the airport over an hour ago. I was getting off one plane and I saw her with a bag, getting on another. She didn't see me, but I saw her."

"She was by herself?"

"Yes why?"

Where the hell was she going?

And without my brother and her kids?

Suddenly, I remembered what she'd said about the dream not being a dream at all.

I looked at Polo suspiciously.

"Who is Vanessa Polo?"

He looked at me emotionless.

"Who?"

"Vanessa!"

"I don't know a Vanessa."

Liar!

Sure I'd mentioned the dream eventually to Micki but I'd never given her too many specifics.

But it was something about the way she'd said it.

She'd said it like it was the truth and like she felt that she might as well tell me since she had gotten the money and planned on getting missing.

"You're lying to me!"

"No I'm not. I don't know any Vanessa."

I rolled my eyes at him.

"Oh how I missed you."

"Polo don't start your shit. I'm married to your best friend again so step off!"

"I know that. Damn. But I still missed you."

Polo acted as though his feelings were hurt and without saying anything more he drove in one direction, and I drove in the other.

It was time to get the truth out of Eddie.

Once and for all.

I got home to find Eddie and the kids outside.

"I was starting to think that you had forgotten how to get home," he said.

"No, I was…"

"Meeting Polo."

Wait…what?

"No."

"So you didn't see Polo?"

"No. I mean yes I did. But not on purpose. I was already sitting there, waiting for Micki and he pulled up. And--,"

Eddie held up his hand.

"I don't want to hear it Sassi. I don't want to hear it," he said, stood up and walked towards his newly leased Suburban.

"Eddie," I said behind him and the boys repeated their father's name but he got into his new car that he'd leased not too long ago and pulled off.

"Damn it!" I screamed.

I didn't even get to ask him about Vanessa again and how did he know that I'd run into Polo?

After loading up the boys, and stopping at the bank to deposit the check, I headed to Mama's to tell her what Micki had said and so we could get in touch and tell him that his wife was on the run.

What the hell are you up to Micki?

~***~

"Who is she?"

"I don't know."

"Who is she Eddie?"

"Damn it! I don't know!"

He screamed in my face but I asked him again.

"I just want to go to sleep Sassi. Can I do that? Damn!"

He got so defensive when it came to this subject, which made me believe even more that he was lying.

"Tell me who she is? Is she someone from your past? Was she your mistress? Did Polo do something to her? Did he kill her? What? And how did Micki know about it?"

Eddie groaned.

It had been over a week since anyone had seen or heard from Micki.

It was safe to say, that she was probably gone.

And she'd left her kids and her husband behind.

I couldn't help but wonder if she'd planned it all exactly the way that it'd happened. I couldn't help but wonder where she was. But I knew in my heart, I could tell in her voice, that she wasn't coming back.

Ever.

We both were set for the rest of our lives.

Now I had to figure out whether or not Eddie would be living lavish with me.

"Who is she?"

"Ask me that again Sassi. I dare you. Go on, ask me again and I promise that I will walk out that door and never come back. Ask me. I told you. I don't know who Vanessa is. It was a dream. Maybe Micki was pulling your leg. I don't know. Maybe she said it to piss you off or drive you crazy. I don't know! But I don't know who Vanessa is!"

Eddie screamed and turned his back to me.

I guess it could have been a possibility that Micki was just being a bitch, but I was willing to put my bank account on it that she wasn't.

I turned over and quietly, mentally, started to form a plan.

Didn't Eddie know that if a woman wanted to know something, she could find it?

A woman was better than the CIA at finding the truth when there was something that she wanted to know and I was in full investigation mode.

I didn't have to mention it to him anymore, but that damn sure didn't mean that I was going to stop looking.

I was going to find out who Vanessa was or is; even if I had to play dirty to do it. And by playing dirty I was sure that meant that I was going to have to do some playing with Polo.

Polo would break before Eddie would. I was sure of it. So, Eddie could blame himself for what I was about to do next. My next actions were his fault and his problem.

Not mine.

****

Chapter 6

Of course I was forbidden to see Polo and I was sure that if Eddie found out that I was trying to find a way to see him, he was going to go insane. I would say that I didn't care, but just in case there was a small chance that Micki had been just starting trouble, I didn't want to completely mess things up with Eddie and I.

I still wasn't sure if he'd believed that Polo just happened to ride by and see me at Micki's, but he had been mad for about a week before he let it go. But he did tell me that he would be watching and that I had better not be trying to play him or hurt him again.

So though I wanted to get in touch with Polo, I didn't want to call him because I was sure that Eddie was checking up on things now that he knew that Polo was back in town.

Maybe Polo felt the same way which he would always call me private. Either way, I had to find a way to see him.

Eddie loved me, but so did Polo.

And the difference between Polo and Eddie was that Polo was unstable; which meant after so long it seemed as though he always got tired of lying and pretending and which also meant that I had a better chance and breaking him down and getting the truth out of him, than I had with Eddie.

We had finally been able to touch the money and with so much of it, we didn't know what to do with it first.

And to be honest, I wasn't exactly focused on spending it.

I was focused on the truth.

Nevertheless I was taking Mama a million dollars and I was going to give my brother some money too once I was able to get in touch with him. Mama told me that Micki had come one day and took the kids from school, so they were gone with her, wherever she was. Mama said he'd gone to pick them up, and was told that their mother signed them out, but she hadn't been at home when he'd got there.

Maybe she never left. Or maybe she did and figured out that she couldn't live without her little brats and came back for them. Either way, Micki and her kids were gone and she'd left my brother, her new husband, in the wind, and he wasn't taking it too well.

I pulled up at Mama's house with the check in my hand.

Her car was there, but there was also a car that I didn't recognized. I figured that one of her old, gossiping friends had gotten a new car, so not thinking much of it I used my key to try to get in but I was stopped by the chain on the door.

"Ma, why is the chain on the door?" I yelled, peeking through the crack.

And I damn near went blind from what I saw.

Mama's bare ass was up in the air and she was on her knees, giving head to some man that was lying on his back on the floor.

Oh, oh, here it comes!

I gagged so loud that it damn near scared both of them to death.

"Ugh!"

Mama yelled for me to close the door and I did as I was told and had a seat on the porch. That had to be the nasty thing I'd ever seen in my life! And I do mean ever!

After a while, Mama came out in her robe.

"Why didn't you call first?"

"I never call first. And neither do you remember?"

How? When?

I hadn't seen Mama with any other man other than my daddy. Like ever.

I had no idea that she was dating and she never so much as mentioned seeing another man.

And she was having sex? And giving head?

Now that was just plain ole' nasty!

I was going to be sick. I focused on sitting still.

"What is it Sassi?"

"Why didn't you tell me that you were seeing someone?"

"Because it's none of your business. What do you want?"

She was still trying to catch her breath.

"Who is he?"

"No one that I want to introduce. He's just Mama's little friend. Now. What is it?"

Still trying to erase the visual of her on her knees from my memory, I stood up and reached her the check.

"Thanks for being my Mama," was all I said and she smiled. I left her and her company to finish whatever foolishness they called themselves doing, and I hurried back home to tell Eddie about what I saw.

"Eddie she was giving head," I frowned but he was dying laughing.

"Well, maybe you should get her to give you a lesson or two. Tell her we will pay her for her head...I mean her time," Eddie burst into laughter as I started to chase him through the house.

Eww! Just eww!

~***~

I had been trying to conveniently be in a few places that Polo might go.

I needed to run into him. I couldn't call him and I couldn't go by his house. Eddie was keeping his eye on me more than the usual lately and anytime we weren't in each other's presence, he was blowing my phone up.

But if anybody knew something, Polo did. And I could make him tell me.

Eddie had run out to get a few more things before our big trip the next day. We were taking the kids on their first vacation of many.

Eddie of course let his job go and was trying to figure out what kind of company he could start to keep income flowing and coming in for years to come and even something that our kids could one day inherit.

He was thinking that maybe we could start a chain of laundromats or something like that but he hadn't exactly finished all of the calculations on it.

Things between us were fine; at least that's what he thought. I was still trying to find out the truth. I hadn't asked him about Vanessa again. There was no point because he wasn't going to tell me.

But I was still looking for answers.

With Eddie gone and the kids watching a movie, I carried a few things out to put in the truck since we would be driving.

My second load, I noticed Polo's car, just passing by.

Yes!

"Polo! Polo! Polo!"

Though it was crazy that he was still riding by, at that moment, I didn't care.

He was just the man that I needed to see. Waving my arms, he slammed on brakes.

I looked at my phone.

I knew that Eddie would call once he left the store, just like he always did, so just in case, I needed to talk fast.

"Still riding by I see?"

"I always watch you."

Yeah, yeah, I know.

"Polo, who is Vanessa?"

"I don't know Sassi. Where are y'all going?"

"Eddie didn't tell you?"

"No."

I wondered if it was for a reason, but with the entire trunk filled with luggage, it wasn't like I could lie.

"Florida. We're driving there tomorrow."

"Oh."

"Polo, I really need to know who Vanessa is. I need to know what she has to do with Eddie."

"I don't know."

"Please Polo. Please," I tried begging him.

My phone started to ring and I saw it was Eddie.

"You have to go."

"See you in Florida," Polo said and drove away.

What?

"Hello," I answered the phone for my husband as I watched Polo's car until it was out of sight.

Did Polo just say that he was coming to Florida?

Just as he said that he would, Polo was in Florida.

I'd spotted him, keeping a distance from us as we checked in at the hotel.

Usually, I would be frustrated by his need to always be somewhere lurking, and watching, but this time I was glad that he was close by. I could definitely find some time to get some distance away from Eddie so that I could talk him.

Eddie seemed to be in a great mood and though I wanted to join him in high spirits and just be happy, I couldn't focus on much until I knew what it was that he was keeping from me.

So for now, I was pretending just like everyone in my circle often did so well. I was being the perfect wife, wearing the perfect smile and making sure that my husband thought that everything was perfect.

But it wasn't.

The drive had us all worn out so we took a much needed nap. Hours later, we headed out to sight see. It had been a while since we'd gone anywhere and despite the other things on my mind, I allowed myself to have some fun and make a few family memories.

"I love you Sassi," Eddie said.

"I love you too." I really did.

But I knew there was something that he was keeping from me.

A private call caused my phone to buzz.

Eddie and the kids were getting settled at the restaurant and I excused myself to the bathroom.

I waited for the call to call again.

And as always, it did.

"Hello?"

"You look so beautiful today," Polo said.

"You really followed us here?"

"You needed me," he said.

"How do you figure that?"

"It was in your voice. I'm in the penthouse suite at the same hotel you guys are staying at."

"I need to talk to you Polo."

"Well, come and talk to me," he said and he hung up the phone.

I made my way back out to Eddie and enjoyed the rest of our dinner. After another hour or two, we finally made our way back to the hotel. I'd been internally plotting on the perfect excuse to get away from my husband.

Spotting a lingerie store on the way in, I'd found one.

"Get the kids bathed and in bed and be waiting for me when I get back. We passed a store and I think I saw something that I might want to wear for you later," I flirted with Eddie once we were back in our room.

Of course I wasn't really going to a store, but Eddie didn't have to know that. I would simply say that they didn't have my size when I came back empty handed.

"I knew there was a reason that you wanted all of this room. I should have known that you had plans to be nasty," Eddie said, kissed my lips, and handed me the car keys.

"And don't go to sleep Eddie. Put the boys to bed. Not yourself," I teased as he chuckled.

"You better hurry up then."

I headed back out of the room and took the elevator to the top floor. I called the hotel lobby and asked for Polo's room, just to make sure.

After getting confirmation, I knocked on the door.

"It's about time, I'm starving," Polo said as he opened the door. "Oh. I thought you were room service," he said, moving out of the way so that I could come inside.

His room was amazing!

Eddie and I had gotten a great room, just because, but it had nothing on Polo's.

It was extravagant, and fit for a king.

We still had to get used to spending like folks did that had a whole lot of money. We hadn't gotten the hang of being wasteful yet.

"So," he said.

"I can't believe you came all the way here," I said, taking a seat in one of the chairs.

"I don't see why you would be surprised. Even when I'm not around, I'm still around. Besides, I get the feeling that you wanted me here," Polo walked closer to me.

My body tensed.

"Move. I only want to know what you know about Vanessa."

"Why are you so obsessed with some woman that you don't even know?"

"So you're admitting that she does exist?"

"No. I'm just curious."

"I wasn't dreaming was I Polo? Micki told me that I wasn't dreaming. That Vanessa really does exist. She was telling the truth wasn't she? What did y'all do to me huh? What you knocked me out and then you guys staged it to look like I was dreaming?"

A knock on the door came and my heart started to race.

"Room service," the lady on the other side of the door said.

Of course it wasn't Eddie, but you never know.

Polo paid for his things and came back to join me.

"I can't love him like I should, feeling like there's something that I don't know," I said to Polo.

"There will always be something that you don't know Sassi," he said eating a strawberry.

"That's the problem. What do I have to do for you to tell me who she is Polo?"

"I don't know who she is Sassi."

"But you're lying."

"Prove it."

That's the problem, I couldn't.

Polo walked closer to me again and sat beside of me with the bowl of strawberries in his hand.

"Take a bite baby," Polo said reaching a strawberry in my direction.

"I'm not your baby Polo. You got what you wanted. Eddie and I remarried and we're fine."

"Then stop snooping and just be fine then."

Polo was right.

Maybe I should just sweep this Vanessa situation under the rug too. But I just didn't want to.

"You sure you don't want a bite?"

"I don't want no damn strawberry Polo!"

"Fine. You don't have to be so nasty about it. And you've been gone long enough. Maybe you should get back," he said to me.

"He thinks that I went to the store," I said to him.

"No. He thinks that you came to find me," Polo said.

"What? He doesn't even know you're here. Right?"

"He knows that I'm probably not too far away. He knows me. And I know him. You should get back."

Polo stood and so did I.

There was no doubt in my mind that they had done something to me and I was positive that they were all trying to cover up something. I didn't know how Micki tied into it all but I was sure that there was something about the truth that I wasn't going to like.

Could I live with the truth was the question.

I sure as hell didn't feel like I could live without it. Without knowing the truth.

"Polo just tell me the truth."

"The truth is he loves you. I love you. And that's the truth. Eddie is about to call you," he said.

I walked out of the room and just as I reached the elevator, my phone started to ring.

It was Eddie.

Well I'll be damned!

~***~

I watched Mama call, but I didn't press ignore. She would have known that I'd sent her to the voicemail. She still wouldn't tell me who her new *boo* was but in a way I was just glad that she was finally getting her groove back. She hadn't been happy, or in love in such a long time. Patrice had stolen that from her. And now she had a chance to get it back, so I wasn't going to complain about it.

Mama left a voicemail, but I didn't even bother to check it. I was too busy thinking about other things. Translation: I was too busy trying to figure out how to find Vanessa.

I scanned Eddie's calls online for the third time that week None of them were out of the ordinary. Most of them were to me or to Polo. He never so much as mentioned Polo to me again and I dared not say anything about him.

Mama called a few more times until finally she gave up and I headed to mess in some of Eddie's things. It wasn't that I believed he was a bad person or that he and I shouldn't be married to him or that we shouldn't be back together. But I did believe that there was something about him and maybe even Polo that was important and that I needed to know.

I'd gone all of these years without knowing, but maybe that was the problem with our relationship all along. And maybe curiosity kills that cat, but I just needed to know, for my own sanity. And who knows, maybe even for my own safety.

Of course we'd found the perfect house to purchase with the money that I'd gotten from Patrice. Everything was packed and even the things that we'd had in storage had been sitting in the living room for the last two days, waiting for the movers to come and take it over to our new place.

I started to go through some of the boxes. Especially those that had most of Eddie's things in them. I wasn't looking for anything in particularly. But you never know what you might come across if you actually go looking. I came across some old photos. Some of them were from when we'd first started dating. We looked so happy. I was smiling as though I'd hit the jackpot and I was holding on to Eddie as though I was afraid to let him go. Eddie looked genuinely happy standing beside me. And I'm sure that he was.

I smiled as I looked at the wedding photos; the ones from over ten years ago. I could see nothing but love in Eddie's eyes. But even I seemed to be so happy but it was nothing more than a painted smile. I was scared. I was terrified of the future. And in my mind, I knew that I'd just made a huge mistake. But yet I smiled. I smiled as though I didn't have a care in the world, but behind that smile, I wanted to cry.

After glancing at Eddie in the photo once more, something made me look over at the face of his best man's...Polo. I noticed that he wasn't smiling. He didn't crack a smile in one single picture. I never noticed that before. I also noticed the look of disgust that seemed to be on Patrice's face in a few of them. I put the pictures away and kept digging up memories. I came across my senior year high school yearbook. I smiled at the photos of Patrice and I. I till you, we just knew that we were the shit back then. Patrice had refused to go to a charter school, even though her family had money. She'd always wanted to go to school with me. She'd always said that she just wanted to be a normal kid.

I beamed at our senior photos. We were young and boy was I sexy. I remembered thinking that I had my whole life ahead of me as I walked across that stage. I was ready for the world and I just wanted to be great.

At that moment I felt like I'd wasted a lot of time. I felt as though my whole life had passed me by without me actually living and enjoying it. But it was time to start. The thoughts of happily ever after almost made me not want to continue investigating Eddie. I had more than enough money now to do anything that I wanted to do. I could finally see the world. I could finally try new things and never have to worry about bills or whether or not I had enough money or not. I could finally live a life like Patrice did. The life that I'd always envied.

I should just be thankful, grateful for all of life's second chances instead of trying to find a reason to second guess.

Though I was deep in thought about completely forgetting about it all, I picked up Eddie's senior photos and his yearbook. I swear he still looked the same. He was still as handsome today as he was twenty years ago. I opened his yearbook to look at him and Polo senior pictures. They were even voted Most Likely to remain Best Friends of their senior class nominations. You could just tell that they were as close as two butt cheeks just by looking at the photo. For some reason as I studied it, Eddie seemed to be the weird and sneaky one, whereas Polo seemed to be the one that was calm, cool and collected.

The lies a photo could tell.

I started to close the book but taking one last glance at the page, something caught my eye.

Stella.

I saw that on the same page "Class Clown" of Eddie's senior class went to a girl named Stella Jackson.

I flipped to find her senior picture.

She was cute and actually she looked just like the girl, her younger sister, from the grocery store that revealed to me that Eddie had paid her sister to put the drugs in my purse.

I went to search the back of the book. I wanted to see if she had signed it or left some type of comment like most seniors do.

She had.

Hey Eddie,

My favorite guy! We had a heck of a year huh? Anyways see you later. And maybe even forever. XOXO, Stella.

So they'd dated maybe? In high school?

He'd never mentioned her to me, ever, so if they were still in contact, why wouldn't he?

And how had he convinced her to do what she had done to me?

I wondered if I should mention her to Eddie, but I decided that there wasn't any reason to. He probably wouldn't tell me the truth about her anyway. Whatever I wanted to find out, I was going to have to find it on my own.

I closed the box and instead of going through another one, I headed to take a seat.

Sassi, just let it be. Move on. Be happy. The past is the past.

Internally, I coached myself to stop looking for trouble because if trouble wanted to find me, I was sure that it would. It damn sure had never gotten lost on its way to my house before.

Just as I'd convinced myself that I was done playing detective, a private number called my phone and I was sure that it was probably Polo.

He didn't bother me all the time, not like he used to, but every now and then he would call and say he just needed to hear my voice. I was past seeing it as strange. Polo was strange.

Point. Blank. Period.

Even though I knew I should probably stop answering his calls, I always answered them anyway.

"Hello?"

"So if I know you, and I do, you're hunting for Vanessa," she said.

Micki.

I couldn't believe that it was her.

No one had seen or heard from her since she up and disappeared.

"Where are you?"

"Living."

"You drop a bomb on me and just disappear."

"You needed closure."

"Closure? Your confession didn't give me closure at all. It's been driving me crazy if anything trying to find answers."

"You need answers? I have those. But you have had them all along. You just don't know it."

What did she mean by that?

"So it wasn't a dream?"

"No."

"And there really is a Vanessa?"

"Yes."

"And the pregnancy. Did I just happen to lose the baby or did someone do something to me?"

"You know Polo has connections with pills and pharmacies. Remember, he got those pills for Eddie? Who knows where he got the pills from. Anyway, he gave you something to make you lose the baby while you were passed out. You even woke up a little as he put the pill in your mouth and put water behind it to make you swallow it. He had to make you pass out again. Do you remember? You woke up for just a second. Remember?"

What! He did what? And hell no I didn't remember it! I didn't remember anything other than the very beginning until I woke up again.

"My guess is that he'd learned a few tricks from some woman that he used to screw to assist with you passing out and all. I've heard that there are certain pressure points that can do that you know," she said. " And as for the pill that he gave you, I guess it was like some kind of abortion pill or something. You know they make those these days. Times have surely changed. They ran out and replaced the tests and all of the good stuff. To make it look like a dream. If you couldn't prove that you were awake, they could surely plant the proof to make it look like you were dreaming."

You have got to be kidding me!

"Why?"

"Why was it done? Or why am I telling you now?"

"Both," I said.

"Well, some secrets are meant to be kept and you are just a little too nosey for your own good. You've always been that way. And why did I tell you, well, you know I never could hold water. I know your husband better than you do. And I also know you, better than you think. I know you well enough to know that you are there about to mess up your marriage because I opened my big mouth and told you that you weren't dreaming. Maybe that was my mistake. I always did talk too much. I think that's why you liked me. I would say the things that you wouldn't say. And do the things you were afraid to do. But if I know you, and I do, you are digging and you shouldn't be Sassi. You are safe with Eddie. He loves you. And he would never let anything happen to you. He has a past, but don't we all? I do. You do. Everyone does. Let it go and be happy."

"You are one to be giving out marital advice," I said slyly.

"It's no secret that I wanted the money. I was running out of options and real love was running away from me. I saw an opportunity and I took it. But I got the money. I'm gone now, and I'm never coming back. I was supposed to be leaving a little while ago anyway."

"Why? Why were you supposed to be leaving?"

"That's neither here nor there. Just know that I had to go and I'll never be coming back Sassi. But you have a chance at new beginnings. Digging around will only hurt you in the end. Just let it go and be happy. For once just be happy. That's what I plan to do."

I was going to take her advice, but since she was on the phone, there was one thing that I just had to ask her. I needed to know just one thing.

"Okay, say I take your advice. Say I stop looking. Will you tell me one thing. Who is she?"

"Who Vanessa?"

"Yes. That's all I want to know. And I'll leave it all alone. Who is she?" I asked Micki again.

"Sassi. She was my sister," Micki said and with that, she was gone.

Wait a minute…what!

****

Chapter 7

Now that I was sure that Eddie, Polo and Micki had been lying to me, I had the worst attitude ever! I tried not to. I tried to let it go but it was so hard!

I didn't want Eddie to touch me. I barely had two words to say to him on most days. All I could think about was that he was a liar and that he was hiding this Vanessa woman from me for a reason, and I wanted to know why.

Replaying Eddie's comments to Polo that day over and over again in my head, I could only assume that this Vanessa woman was dead and the fact that Micki said "was" confirmed it.

Did Polo kill her?

Did he kill her for Eddie?

And if so, how did Micki find out? Well, if it was her sister she would know that she was dead, but why wouldn't she tell me about her? And why would they all be trying to keep it a secret?

"Hey baby," Eddie said as I shut my laptop.

I was trying to give him a fake smile but it was hard for me not to pretend that I wasn't bothered.

"What's wrong with you?"

"Nothing."

"Give me some shugga'."

I stared at him.

"See, there is something wrong. What are you…"

"No Eddie. I'm not cheating if that's what you were going to ask. I'm not doing anything. I would never hurt you again."

"Well what is it?"

"I just have some questions," I mumbled.

Eddie exhaled loudly.

"You told me you that didn't know a Vanessa," I started.

"What? Here we go with this again bull crap Sassi," Eddie said in disgust.

"Who is she?" Just tell me who she is? I know that I wasn't dreaming that night."

He stuttered for a second but quickly pulled himself together.

"I don't know a Vanessa."

"Well do you know a Stella?"

I saw fear in Eddie's eyes, but he sat right there and lied anyway.

"No."

Liar!

"Really? She signed you yearbook and from the looks of it you guys were close."

"My yearbook? From 20 years ago Sassi? Really? And now that you mentioned it, yes, I went to school with a Stella. Haven't seen her in years. We were friends. Well, not really friends, but friendly. Stop looking for something to be wrong Sassi. You've always been nosey. One day you are going to stick your nose in business where it doesn't belong and someone is going to knock it the hell off."

Whatever. I wasn't all that nosey. Not all the time anyway.

Eddie walked off and yelled for me to follow him but I ignored him.

I opened my laptop again instead.

If only I could find out what happened to Vanessa...

~***~

Eddie grunted and released himself inside of me.

Sex between us was still better than it had been in years and now that sex was no longer an issue, I'd found plenty more things that concerned me about him.

Maybe I was the only one that noticed, but Eddie was still a little odd. He wasn't the same man as he had been before the affair between Polo and I. I always found myself watching him. The way that he talked, walked, and even down to the way he dressed. He just seemed different.

I would have liked to have taken Micki's advice and just let it all go and leave whatever it was in the past, but I just couldn't stop thinking about it. I'd tried calling her old number back, but of course it was disconnected and being that she'd called me private, I had no way to reach her.

And Vanessa was her sister?

How?

I'd always known Micki to be the oldest of three siblings.

Micki was from out of town and moved here in her teens with her grandmother once her mother passed away. Her other two siblings had the same father, and they had gone to live with their dad, so she had stayed around, with little family, even after her grandmother was long gone.

Patrice and I had been friends, first, since we were roughly twelve years old. She was the sister that I'd never had. As we got older, and because Patrice was into everything, anything that her father could stick her in; girl scouts, cheerleading, gymnastics, she'd done it all, she always met other friends. It was her father's way of keeping her busy, her mind off of losing her mother too I suppose.

One summer at summer camp, Patrice met Micki. Her and Micki became close and as the summer ended, they stayed in touch, and then Patrice introduced me to Micki. I tried to remember exactly when, but I was thinking that I we were all around sixteen years old then when Micki officially became a "best friend" too.

Ever since then, she'd been around and until here lately, she had been nothing but loyal. She'd always had my back and she'd always been there for me to count on in a loud, crazy sort of way, but nevertheless, she'd always been right there.

So if Vanessa was her sister, that would have meant that she was older than Micki and must have died before Patrice and I had met her.

But how?

And why hadn't anyone ever mentioned her before?

Micki had never, not even once, mentioned her and there were no pictures of her, anywhere that I'd ever been with Micki.

I found that more than strange.

If this Vanessa woman was her real sister, than why did she and everyone pretend like she didn't exist?

As Eddie started to snore, I entertained my thoughts a little more. There had to be some twisted situation involving all of them and the truth to the matter was that it was probably in my best interest if I didn't know about it.

Unable to sleep, I left Eddie to rest and tip-toed out of our huge bedroom. We were in the new house now, and it was beautiful. It was my dream home and it was more than I'd ever imagined that it'd be. The boys loved all of the space and Eddie was looking forward to making tons of new memories here. But it was just so hard for me to focus on forever when I had so much more on my mind.

It was late summer, so I headed outside.

It was two o'clock in the morning, but it was still hot and sticky. I tightened my robe and took a seat. I looked around at all of the beautiful, gigantic houses that belonged to our new neighbors. I hadn't had the pleasure of meeting any of them yet, but I was looking forward to. I was going to enjoy meeting new people and even possibly making new friends. Hell, I had two friendship slots currently available anyway.

Thinking about Patrice, I wondered if she knew about Vanessa too. I was willing to bet that she did. They all seemed to know more than enough about each other and no one ever bothered to tell me.

What was with all of the secrecy?

The headlights stole my attention and immediately, my gut told me that the headlights belonged to one of Polo's cars.

I was right.

He turned off his lights and creeped past my house, not knowing that I was sitting there on the porch, watching him. Once he made it to the stop sign and the end of the street, he sat there for a long while.

I wished that I hadn't left my phone inside of the house. I would have taken that risk of calling him just so that I could tell him to take his stalking ass home and go to bed. After a few more minutes, finally, he flicked back on his lights and he made a turn.

I watched his car until it was out of sight. I thought about Polo and the things that he'd said. He'd said that he'd always watched me. Even when I didn't know it, he'd said that he'd always watched me.

How could anybody be that obsessed over someone yet not only help their best friend marry her the first time around, but then go away in hopes of helping his best friend marry the same woman of his dreams...again?

It just didn't make sense.

Sure he cared about him, but if he loved me that much, why was he so willing to let Eddie have me? There had to be something more.

Why couldn't I see it? Why couldn't I figure it out?

Shaking away my thoughts, I headed back inside. But just as I shut the door, I noticed lights coming down the road again, and just like last time, just as he approached the house, Polo turned them off. I watched Polo slowly creep by again as I locked the door and headed back to lie in bed beside of Eddie. For some strange reason, and as crazy as it might sound, a part of me felt just a little safer, knowing that Polo was always somewhere watching.

But the other part of me knew that there had to be another reason why.

~***~

I sat in the car and looked at Mama and Patrice's lawyer head into a restaurant. The same restaurant that I'd just ordered take-out from. They were hand and hand and he'd even patted her on the booty while she smiled.

Mama was dating Patrice's lawyer?

Since when?

I wondered if he had been the one that she was servicing with her mouth, more or less, that day that I'd popped up at her house.

Why wouldn't she tell me that she was dating him?

Had they been dating before or after Patrice died?

He'd certainly never mentioned even knowing my mother during our visits for him to read the Patrice's will.

Hmmm...

I called Eddie to let him know that I was on my way home with the food. I was hoping that he found something to get his hands into soon because we definitely needed some kind of space or outlets from each other on a daily basis. He was getting on my last nerve and I knew that I was getting on his, though I knew exactly were my impatience and frustration was coming from.

Instead of calling Mama and asking her a hundred questions, I pulled off and headed down the road towards my house. I pulled up just in time to see a black car pulling off. I didn't recognize it and I couldn't see who was driving it as they drove away.

"Eddie who was that?" I asked walking into the house.

"Who was who?"

"Outside? In the black car that just left?"

Eddie grabbed the food out of my hands.

"I don't know babe. What they say? Were they here? At our house?"

"Yes. They pulled off as I pulled up."

"Oh. They didn't come here. Maybe they had the wrong address or something," he said taking a bite of his food.

Humph.

Here lately, I didn't believe a word that Eddie said and I was starting to rethink my decision. My husband didn't feel like was my husband at all.

Had he planned on remarrying me again all along?

Was all of this some kind of plan or set up?

Did I make the mistake and marry the wrong husband…again?

~***~

"Meet me," I said to Polo.

"Where?"

I tried to think of somewhere simple; somewhere where it would seem as though we just happened to run into each other instead of sneaking around to meet without Eddie's knowledge or permission.

"Hell, the grocery store I guess. I'll be there in ten minutes," I said to Polo.

I hung up, erased the private call and headed to the backyard.

"Get in the pool with us babe," Eddie said.

He was now sitting on the edge of it. Eddie could swim like a fish and looking at the water dripping off of his body, I thought about what Polo had told me about Eddie saving his life and keeping him from drowning.

"Okay, but after I run to the store to get some steaks for the grill," I said to Eddie.

"Oh, steaks would be good. Get some shrimp too," he said.

I blew him a kiss and he caught it with a smile.

Bastard.

I still loved him, sure, but he couldn't fool me. I didn't have to be a genius to know that he was going the extreme to make sure that whatever he was hiding, stayed hidden.

I just wanted the truth. Was that too much to ask for?

I sped to the grocery store. Polo was already there and once I started to head in, he got out of his car and followed a small distance behind me. I headed to the meat section and he walked up.

"Hey beautiful."

Oh my. I accidentally blushed.

"I found out who Vanessa is, or was, or whatever," I said to him.

"Oh really?" he said.

Wait a minute.

My mind started to wonder. I was doing all of this confiding in Polo, when he was obviously in on it all and lying to me too. And on top of all of that, he could be telling Eddie every single thing that I told him. After all, they were loyal to each other before they were loyal to anyone else.

I'd learned that the hard way.

"You know what, never mind. You probably tell him everything I tell you anyway," I said to Polo, grabbed a few steaks, and turned to walk away.

But Polo grabbed my arm.

"No. I don't. I don't," Polo said looking into my eyes.

Maybe he didn't. Probably because he often told me things that he wasn't supposed to tell me anyway.

"You lied to me Polo."

"Sometimes I have to."

"Well, what happened to her? Did you kill her or something? And she's Micki's sister? Or she was? Like who is this woman?"

"What? Uh…wait did you say something about Micki? Who told you that she was Micki's sister?"

"I've been doing some digging," I lied.

He looked like he didn't believe me. I could tell that he had his guard up but I could also tell that he was about to tell me something that I probably didn't want to hear.

"If I tell you that I killed her will you leave it alone? Well, I guess I just did," Polo said.

What? He killed her?

"You killed who? Vanessa? You're saying that you killed her Polo? Like actually killed her? Why? Was it for Eddie?"

"No and it's something that I'm not proud of. It was an accident. Now that is the truth. Let it go okay and just be happy with Eddie and the kids and stuff," Polo said.

I still felt like there was more to the story and I wanted it all.

"So Eddie knows this?"

"Of course."

"Why did you do it?"

"It was an accident."

"Why didn't you go to jail?"

"It was an accident."

"Who was she? To Eddie?"

"They kind of dated back in the day."

"How did she die?"

"I accidentally backed up as she was walking behind the car. The bump knocked her down and her head hit the pavement. She died."

Hmm…

Sounded like bullshit to me!

"Why are you lying?"

"I'm not lying. I accidentally killed Vanessa."

"What's her last name so I can look it up for myself."

"What? You don't need her last name. I'm telling you who she is and what happened to her right now."

"Why were you denying it at first? Why did you all keep it a big secret? Why wouldn't Micki tell me something like that had happened to her sister? Why did you try to make it like I was dreaming?"

"Because you shouldn't even know about her in the first place. You should stop being so nosey."

"So I keep being told that lately."

"As I told you before, some things in the past Sassi are meant to stay there. For your own good. For your own safety.

It's over and done with. I told you the truth. I killed her, accidentally. Not Eddie."

"Why Polo?"

"I just told you it was an accident."

There was more to it. I could feel it in my bones.

"And she was Micki's sister?"

"Huh? Oh. Yeah. She was. Yes."

"So everyone knew this the whole time but me?"

"Yes."

"And so I hadn't been dreaming at all?" I asked, already knowing the answer but just to clarify.

Polo breathed.

"No."

"You knocked me out?"

"Yes."

"And you made me take some kind of pill to kill the baby?"

"Yes."

Well, at least he was finally being honest.

"And Eddie let you do this to me?"

"Yes. You woke up, looked me right into the eyes as I put the pill in your mouth and the water to get it done your throat. I had to knock you out again. Eddie was going crazy knowing that you were pregnant. He knew before you even took the test. He said that he could just tell. He'd found the pregnancy test days before you took it. He couldn't have handled you having a baby by his best friend. Even if it was his, in his mind, he was convinced that it was mine. It was wasn't it?" Polo asked.

I was still trying to sort out my thoughts but I answered him anyway.

"Probably. Possibly. I'd had sex with Eddie too. Only days a part," I said ashamed.

"Well, it was for the best. Eddie and I have a strong bond, but that would have been a lot to bounce back from and besides a baby meant that you and him wouldn't have been able to work it out and move forward. Well, if the baby was mine. And I just wouldn't have been able to live with myself knowing that I'd let my ways and my wants ruin my brother's marriage," he said.

Polo was different too. Still weird, but yet different.

It was as though he'd somewhat matured overnight or something. As if he wasn't as crazy as he'd always seemed. Or it could have been that he really did care more about Eddie and his happiness, than he cared about his own. Whatever it was, it was almost as though Eddie had changed in a way that made me somewhat uncomfortable and suspicious. And Polo seemed to have changed in a way that made me want to know a little more about this mysterious side to Polo that Eddie told me about; which didn't seem so bad at all.

"You asked about Vanessa, so I just told you about Vanessa. Now you can move on Sassi."

I felt overwhelmed all of a sudden. My mind was racing and I remembered something else that I wanted to ask.

"Did you kill that woman? In the hit and run? The woman that told me that you had taped us having sex. Did you kill her too? For telling me?"

Polo shook his head.

"No."

"Then who did? If you didn't do it, did you pay someone else to do it or something?"

"No."

"Then who did it then? I'm sure that it wasn't just a coincidence."

Polo exhaled.

"This is a stupid question."

"So you do know something then? About the accident?"

"Ugh! Why do you feel the need to want to know everything Sassi?"

"It's a simple question. I just want to know the truth of what's going on around me and how the people around me are involved. Do you know who hit her or not?"

"Fine. If you insist. It was Micki."

What?

"She hit her. She wasn't paying attention to the road. She hit her, panicked and drove away. I saw the whole thing because I had been following her. Not Micki, Katrina was her name. One of my sex buddies. She knew that I was heated about her running her mouth to you and she wouldn't take any of my calls. I was following her to confront her and I saw the accident. I saw Micki hit her, get out of the car to check on her and then drive away. You want to know my involvement? I helped Micki out a little by wiping her prints from the door handle where she'd opened the door, and by cleaning up pieces left behind by the car that she was driving. I owed her a favor anyway."

"What kind of favor?"

"It's not important."

"Micki wasn't too fond of you so what kind of favor? I thought that you were the one that had done a favor for her and you wanted her to repay you with ass. She told me about whatever it was between you two."

"Trust me. There was nothing real between Micki and I. Ever. I was always looking for someone to replace what I feel for you, but trust me, I never looked for it in Micki."

My head was starting to hurt.

"But you did with Patrice?"

"Nope, that one time we came to dinner was just to piss you off like I said."

"So that's why Micki wanted to leave town? So nothing comes back on her for what she did?"

"I guess. Whatever you say."

"And you covered up everything on Micki's behalf?"

"Like I said, I took care of everything so the police will never know who caused the fatal hit and run. And since there was no evidence, I doubt that they are still looking."

I thought back.

"I don't remember Micki's car being wrecked."

"People only remember what they want to remember. Or maybe she made it her business to stay away. Until her car was fixed at least."

Hell, there was no way I could remember how long after the hit run that I'd seen Micki again, so I wasn't even going to try to calculate time and dates to try to convince myself that Polo was really telling the truth. I guess I just had to take his word for it.

"I just find it funny that she'd said that you'd tried to do things to her, crazy things, and then you turnaround and help her cover up something like that."

"I didn't do anything to Micki. So, I don't know what you're talking about. I think you tend to think I'm a little crazier than I actually am. I have my ways, but I'm not crazy. I'm a lot of things, but I'm not crazy."

That depends on his definition of the word. In my mind, he was off and always had been.

"So I guess Micki stayed for her share of the money that we got from the will. The same day she got the money was the day that she left."

Polo shrugged."

"And you didn't kill Patrice did you?"

"Hell no."

"I just thought I would ask."

"Well, I just gave you your answer."

"You've been lying all of this time just like everybody else. Why did you tell me all of this now?"

"To give you a peace of mind. Like I said, I love you Sassi. By now I know that you won't repeat what I tell you, so now that you have what you need, just be happy. More than anything, I want what's best for you. What's best for Eddie."

"And what about what's best for you?"

"I'll figure it out. I always do."

Polo turned to walk away but I grabbed his hand. I hoped that this time he was really being honest with me. I hoped that the things that he'd said were the truth so that I could process them and figure out my next moves.

"Thank you," I said to him.

Polo turned around and without hesitating he kissed me.

"I'll never be too far away," he said and he took one of the steaks out of my head and headed on his way.

I stood there and watched him until he was out of sight.

No I couldn't be with him because he was my husband's best-brother-friend. Or whatever he was. No I couldn't be with him because he had admitted to accidentally as he claimed. Nope, I couldn't be with him because he was an accessory to murder. And I surely couldn't be with him because he was unstable in every way, and on every single level.

But at that moment, in a way I wished that I could. In a way I wished that there were two of me so that Polo and Eddie both could have a part of me. At that moment, I realized that I felt more for Polo than I wanted to, or that I was actually willing to admit, and I was for certain that what Polo felt for me was love; at least some kind of form of it. He didn't show it like most people but I was sure that he loved me to the best of his ability.

But I also knew that no matter what I told myself, no matter what I felt, no matter how attractive Polo was and how good his sex was, there no doubt in my mind that I had a stronger chance with happily-ever after with Eddie than I did with Polo because whether we'd tried now, or had over ten years ago, I was sure that Polo would have been the wrong husband...too.

****

Chapter 8

Since meeting Polo at the store, everything seemed to be better.

I knew Eddie's lies, though he didn't know that I knew, but having some form of the truth did seem to ease my mind. Though I couldn't discuss what Polo had told me with him, it seemed to make me feel better just knowing them. Eddie hadn't really did anything too bad other than be dishonest with me. Polo had been the one to do all of the dirty work. And I wasn't even going to mention Micki and all of the things she conveniently forgot to mention.

I did wonder why she'd lied on Polo though. Why she'd said that she had a feeling that he had been doing crazy things to her and made it like he had been desperately pursuing her. I figured that she was probably trying to scare me and keep me from continuing my affair with him since she'd thought that it was a bad idea from the beginning.

But now that I knew, and now that I was no longer consumed with my thoughts or continuously looking for something, things, Eddie, and our marriage, were better than ever.

There were a few things and thoughts that found their way to my conscious every now and then, but I tried my best not to entertain them. Like why Polo and Eddie, and even Micki had gone through so much trouble to keep what had happened to

Vanessa from me; especially if it was just an accident. And most certainly since Polo had been the one to commit the crime.

So what had been the big deal?

And I often wondered why Micki never mentioned having an older sister that had passed away and why were there no pictures of her. I hadn't asked Polo much about Micki's and Vanessa's sisterhood, but I wished that I had. He hadn't offered the information so maybe he didn't know either, but it still didn't explain why Micki wouldn't have told me something like that, especially about Polo, and especially to detour me from having an affair with him.

It just seemed a little off. But whether it was the whole truth or at least part of it, I was glad to finally at least know something. So, it was what it was.

Polo was still riding by sometimes and checking Eddie's phone, they were talking all the time and Eddie and the kids often went to visit him. Of course he never suggested that I go along. Most of the time Eddie wouldn't even tell me. I would only find out by reading his text messages or if one of the kids said that they saw Uncle Polo that day.

"Go by and water my plants for me."

"Why?" I asked Mama.

"Because. Me and---me and my friend decided to go on a last minute road trip and we're already right here near the highway, so we're just going to jump on it and get going. We're not even going to pack. We will just pick up clothes as we go," she said.

By friend, I knew that she meant Patrice's lawyer but I didn't say anything.

"Just go do what I said. I'll see you when I get back," Mama said and hung up.

Well, I was glad to see that she was living a little. If she was happy, then I was happy too. So, I guess I could just leave it at that.

I told Eddie where I was going and headed to Mama's to do as I was told. I hadn't been over there since the time I'd popped up to give her the money and some her getting down to business.

Going into the house I noticed that she'd redecorated.

Of course she had a good bit of money to do as she pleased from me and on top of that she still got benefits that were left behind from Daddy. But I could see that she'd been spending her money on bringing a little color and life back into her home.

"Go Mama!" I said aloud.

That penis must be magic! Mama had been so stuck in her ways, for so long, and it was nothing like a new, good piece of wood, to make a woman bend.

I watered her plants and stared at some of the family photos on the wall. I wondered how her life would have been had she stayed with her first husband. That she'd told me about.

Had she not ruined her marriage by sleeping around with Daddy, I could only imagine that she would have probably been happier. That drunk of a father of mine ruined her life.

I headed to look around at the rest of the house, just to see the other improvements. I opened the door that used to be my room. It definitely didn't have a thing that belonged to me in it now. Now it was some kind of theater room or something. And a hell of a nice one might I add. There were two recliners, nice paint, a bar, a huge TV and even a popcorn machine. I smiled as I recalled what few happy, childhood memories I could remember.

I headed to Mama's room next.

Her room of course was rather lavish. It was comfy, cozy, and everything in it screamed expensive. Hell that million dollars that I'd given her was going to be gone in a flash if she kept buying like this. I looked at the clothes and the price tags that were on her bed. I guess she was making up for lost time.

She had a bag full of sexy bras and underwear.

"Eww Ma," I said aloud with a frown as I pulled out a pair of thong panties.

She knew better than that!

I held them as though they weren't brand new and opened up her underwear drawer to put them inside. I noticed a bag in the corner and dropped the panties and picked it up.

Opening it, I pulled out a pair of black gloves.

They were clean, but crumpled together as though they had been worn. There was one other thing in the bag so I pulled it out. Immediately I recognized it.

It was Patrice's necklace.

I gasped.

What the hell was Mama doing with Patrice's favorite necklace? It was the necklace that her mother had given her only months before she'd died. Patrice used to wear it all the time. Not every day; but often.

"You've never been good at following directions," Mama said behind me causing me to jump.

"I was just,"

"Just being nosey. Like always."

"I thought you were on the road?"

"We were but he suggested that we ride up to some of the casinos. I figured that I was probably going to need my license for that," Mama nodded towards her wallet on the dresser.

Mama walked closer to me.

I tried to hide Patrice's necklace.

"Go on. Ask me."

"Why do you have Patrice's necklace? And these gloves?"

Mama stared at me.

"No. Ask me what you really want to ask me Sassi."

So many thoughts were running through my mind but I opened my mouth and asked for the truth.

"Did you kill her?"

"No."

I looked at her.

"Then what's with the gloves and why do you have her necklace Mama?"

Mama walked closer and took the gloves and the necklace out of my hands, grabbed her wallet and headed back towards the door.

"Mama, answer me. If you didn't kill her, who did?"

She looked back at me.

"I didn't kill her. But yes. I know who did," was all she said and she headed out the door.

What!

~***~

Mama promised to explain her comment once she was back in town. No matter how much I begged or even threatened her, she wouldn't tell me and only said that it was a conversation that we would have face to face. So the whole tumor thing really was a lie. Patrice had been killed. And Mama knew who had done it.

But how?

I wasn't sure but I couldn't wait for her to get back and explain herself.

"A penny for your thoughts?" Eddie asked sitting beside me.

"I was just thinking about life. Us. The boys. The money. We're going to be okay aren't we?"

Eddie nodded.

"Yeah. I believe we are."

Eddie kissed me and walked out of the room to answer his phone. It was probably Polo.

I stood up and glanced at my laptop and headed to open it. I headed to my book that I hadn't looked at in quite some time.

The title "The Wrong Husband" was perfect, but for some reason as I read over my work, something was missing. Without thinking twice about it, I deleted every single word of it and started again.

"What's a woman to do when she marries the wrong man? Is it possible that life would have been better if she'd married her husband's best friend?"

I smiled as I finished the sentence. Yeah. That sounds much better.

I smirked as I typed and started from the beginning. I got lost in my words for the next few hours as I put my story, a more embellished version of it on paper.

At the next sentence I giggled to myself.

"His best friend was charming, and fine. And secretly I wanted him to be all mine," I typed.

Hmm...

The truth is the truth. No matter how hard a person tries to deny it.

~***~

"Still following me I see," I said to Polo.

"Uh, I was here first," he said as he waited on his sub.

"Oh yeah. You were huh?"

He didn't say anything for a while.

"Thank you."

"For what?"

"Everything. I know how loyal you are to Eddie, but you are the only one in my circle who tried to explain anything to me. I thought I was losing it for a minute."

Polo breathed and then walked really close.

"No problem."

"Patrice was murdered. Mama knows who did it."

"What?"

"She didn't die from a tumor. The police were suspicious a while ago but they didn't have any proof. But Mama says that she knows."

The look in Polo's eyes said something but I couldn't exactly tell what they said.

"Ride with me," he said.

I looked at him.

"Ride with you where?"

"To my place."

"Uh, no. We both know that isn't a good idea Polo."

"I want to show you something. I promise I won't try to touch you. Unless you want me to," he smirked.

"See, oh no."

"For real."

I smirked at him.

Don't go Sassi, I said to myself.

But I couldn't help but wonder what it was that Polo wanted to show me. I nodded at Polo and he smiled.

Oh shit.

This was a bad idea, I could feel it. But being that Eddie was home with the boys and probably had no plans on coming out, I figured that I could go see whatever it was right quick and come straight back.

"I'm leaving my car. Just in case Eddie decides to ride out or something. Or pop up at your house. I can hide my body; but not my car. Right there and right back Polo."

"You have my word."

We walked out together and a few minutes later we pulled up at Polo's house. Our new house was closer to his.

I rushed him inside and he led me to his bedroom.

"I want you to see something."

He disappeared into his closet for a while and then came back out.

"You know what, you might be right. I may have a few stalker tendencies," Polo joked.

"Tell me something I don't know already," I said bluntly.

"Hey, the first step is admitting that you have a problem. Sassi you are my problem. You have been for years."

I didn't respond to him as he put in the DVD.

"I have a confession. The day at the gas station wasn't the first day that I saw you. I'd saw you once before then. But that day was the day that I fell in love with you and I didn't even know you."

Polo pressed play.

"Originally, I recorded this on my phone and transferred it later on. As I said, I've always been into recording and watching beautiful things. I just found this footage the other day."

It was weird how he made stalking seem almost sweet.

I watched the TV.

I'd gone into the store. I was actually with Patrice.

Of course it was before I'd met Eddie and I seemed to be laughing but I couldn't remember what it was that was so damn funny. The smile on my face was priceless. I had such a glow. It was almost like I was watching someone else and not a video of myself

"I knew you were the one for me the first time I saw you but this day, this moment, at that laugh and at that smile, I felt nothing but adornment. I was actually passing by and saw you and pulled into the store. I sat there and just recorded you so that I could go home and just watch you."

"Polo this is unhealthy. And a little scary."

"You never have to be scared of me. I would never hurt you. I should have an approached you, but I couldn't figure out what to say. It wasn't like I did with other women. Hell, I make it clear what I want from them. Even with my ex-wives, initially, it was just about sex. But I knew with you I would have wanted more, and I didn't know how to approach you or the situation, properly." Polo said.

I heard him. And though it was scary but cute, we were past this already. There was nothing that we could do about the past.

Polo put another DVD in.

It was of my wedding. The first one.

The camera zoomed in and I didn't have that smile or that glow that I had on the other video.

I was frowning more than I was grinning. I looked scared. I looked unsure. Hell, I looked down right sad.

He had the camera close on my face as Eddie and I danced our first dance as husband and wife.

I danced as though I was dancing with a stranger or like I was dancing with the most unpopular boy in high school that smelled but I lost a bet and had to go with him to the prom or something.

I just didn't look happy at all.

"Your face told me that you'd made the biggest mistake of your life. That should have been me. You married the wrong husband Sassi. You should have married me."

I'd never admitted it to him, but I figured that it was about time that I did.

"You're right. I did marry the wrong husband Polo. But at this time in my life, he's just right for me. So, I guess it all worked out just fine. And you wanted us to work it out remember?"

"It wasn't that I wanted you to. It was just what was best. You know if something was to ever happen to Eddie, not saying that it will or anything, but if it did, I wouldn't let the opportunity pass me by again you know that right? I never make the same mistake twice."

He always knew just what to say.

"Polo we've made more than enough mistakes with each other. I 've lost count."

"What we shared wasn't a mistake to me Sassi. It was a dream come true."

Aww.

"Okay. Let's get you back to your car. I just found these tapes the other day and I just wanted you to see them."

"For what?"

"So that you could see you, through my eyes. So you could see what I saw when I looked at you."

"Well where are the copies of us having sex? Let me hold them."

Polo laughed.

"Not a chance in hell," he smirked.

He waited for me to stand and walk towards his bedroom door.

I stopped.

"If something was to ever happen to Eddie, I promise you, my only choice would be you," I said to Polo.

Did I really just say that aloud?

And especially to somebody like Polo. I didn't want to give him any ideas.

Polo touched my back.

I turned around to face him and I beamed at him.

"This is goodbye Polo," I said to him knowing that this was it. Eddie would never allow us around each other and as of this moment the private phone calls and periodic conversations had reached the end.

I was going to invest every ounce of my heart and love into loving Eddic. I'd come into this marriage all wrong and it was finally time to do it right.

Polo kissed me and I allowed his lips to dance with my mine until we both had to come up for air. I smiled at him as we headed out the door.

We didn't so much as speak the whole way back to pick up my car and I didn't look back at him once I was out of his car, and as I heard him drive away.

No more looking back.

I was only going to look forward.

Eddie and I were about to start enjoying ourselves and truly living with no regrets and no restraints. And it was time for me to start loving him with my whole heart and nothing less.

I'd been gone for about two hours and Eddie hadn't even called. I called him but he didn't answer so I headed in that direction.

I started to cry and smile at the same time.

But they were happy tears or maybe tears of relief.

Things were going to be better than ever from now on.

Mama called me and though I'd been waiting for her call so that she could explain her comment, I sent her to the voicemail. I could call her back.

I was trying to get home to Eddie.

My husband. And soon to become my best friend.

"Eddie? Baby? Where you at? Boys?"

The house was quiet. Too quiet to be my house.

Soon Eddie appeared.

"Hey, where are the kids?"

"My mother wanted to get them for a while."

"Oh. Why didn't you call and let me know?"

"I figured you wouldn't mind."

I didn't. But usually Eddie called to at least let me know something like that.

"We are alone for a few hours. Let's do something. Something different," Eddie said pulling handcuffs out of his pocket.

Oh, okay! We hadn't done anything kinky in so long so I was all in.

"I've been a very bad girl daddy. Arrest me."

Eddie pulled my hands in front of me and handcuffed them together.

"I love you Eddie," I said as he sat me down on the couch.

"I love you too Sassi."

Eddie walked out of the room for a second and came back.

"The problem is that I love you too much. Way more than you have ever loved me. That's why I have to do this."

Eddie sat right in front of me on the edge of the coffee table. He was holding a knife.

"Eddie? What's going on? Why do you have a knife?"

"You're just like Vanessa."

Excuse me?

Vanessa?

Did he just admit to knowing Vanessa after denying it all that time?

"What did you say Eddie?"

"You heard me. You're just like her. You are just like Vanessa," Eddie stared into space as he twirled the knife.

Fear started to set in and I tried to wiggle free of the handcuffs, but I knew that wasn't going to happen.

"I'm a good man. But every woman that I love...loves him."

I already knew that he was talking about Polo.

"I tried to give us another chance, but you still love him. I watched you leave with him today and go with him to his house."

Huh?

"The kids wanted ice cream. The ice cream shop right beside the place that you and Polo came out of. When I spotted your car, I was just about to call you until I spotted Polo's too. And then I saw you two walk out together and drive away."

Oh hell.

"Eddie it's not what you think. I swear no sex or anything was involved."

"You smell like him."

"You know being too close to him always makes his scent rub off on you. Nothing happened."

Eddie still didn't look me in the eyes.

"Instead of taking the kids in for ice cream, I followed both of you to his house and once you went inside, I called my mother to get the boys. They didn't need to be here for this. You don't love me Sassi. You love Polo. Just like Vanessa did. And now you're going to end up the same way that she did. Dead."

I started to panic.

"You know she was just using me to get close to Polo. I was nice to her. I treated her like a queen but really she only wanted to get close enough for Polo to take notice of her. She didn't want me at all. She wanted him."

Eddie finally looked at me with eyes that I didn't recognize. They were dark. They were cold.

"Is that why Polo killed her?"

"What? Polo didn't kill her. I did."

"Wait, you killed her?"

"Yes. I killed her."

Huh?

Automatically, I knew that Polo had lied to me just to cover up for Eddie.

"Polo tried to save her but he was too late. Polo has always watched people. That's his weird thing. He and I were roommates at the time. Before you. Before us. Anyway, he had cameras all around the house. Vanessa came to visit one day and I'd been working hard to impress her and make her love me. She had me working for it, but I didn't mind. I thought that she was worth it, but just as we started to kiss she stopped me with a confession. Her confession was that she was really more interested in Polo and not me. She said that he was just more her type and she didn't want to be anything more than my friend. I tried to reason with her but she only wanted to talk about Polo since she'd gotten it off of her chest. Anyway, that wasn't the first time that I'd been in that situation before and I just snapped. I grabbed her by the neck and started choking her. Polo happened to be spying on us, as always, and came running but he was too late. By the time he got my hands off of her neck, she was dead. But he helped me make it look like an accident."

I breathed heavily.

What the hell is Eddie talking about?

"It worked too. He watched enough of that crime stuff and had done enough snooping to where he actually managed to pull it off and save me from prison. I only had to go to that place for a little while."

What?

"What place?"

Eddie smiled.

"Take these cuffs off of me Eddie."

"No Vanessa."

"What? I'm not Vanessa Eddie. I'm Sassi."

"Whatever you say Vanessa ," he said.

Eddie had been the one to kill Vanessa and Polo had covered up for him.

Then thinking about Eddie's statement to Polo on the tape that day, Polo must have killed someone else.

"So if you killed Vanessa," I started.

"You are Vanessa," Eddie said.

I'm not Vanessa!

But obviously he was going crazy or something so I went along.

"If you killed the "other" Vanessa, on the tape why did you ask Polo to do it like last time?"

"Oh. Is that what I said on the tape? I must have misunderstood what you were saying to me back then. I thought you heard me say something about the "other" Vanessa. If I'd said that, then I was talking about my mother. My real one. Polo killed my biological mother for me."

His what?

"I'm not really my parent's son Sassi. They took me in when I was five. The woman that raised me, the woman that you know as my mother, is my aunt. At five, she took me from my mother and raised me as her own. That's when I met Polo."

What!

"So your real mother is dead? Polo killed her?"

"Yes. She's the reason I'm so messed up. I only remember pieces of things that happened while I was with her, but what little I can recall, wasn't good. She was a stripper and prostitute. She loved men. And she hated real life responsibilities. She couldn't even remember who my real father was. Anyway, my aunt and uncle took me in because she couldn't have kids and because she didn't think her sister was the best mother figure for me. But no matter what, I loved her, my real mother, and all I ever wanted was for her to love me back. But she wouldn't. No one ever loved me the way that I loved them. The story of my life."

Eddie wasn't his parent's real child!

You have got to be freaking kidding me!

They had baby pictures of him and everything but I guess they would have considering that they were still his relatives.

I felt so deceived.

"Anyway after the incident with the "other" Vanessa, after a while, I went to find her. Actually Polo had found her for me. I went to see her. It was suggested that maybe I get some kind of closure or try expressing to her how empty I felt to have been unwanted and rejected by my birth mother. But guess what? She barely had two words to say to me. She saw Polo and her whore radar went bananas. She pretty much ignored everything that I said and focused more on trying to get Polo in her bedroom."

"And Polo killed her."

"He knows me better than anybody. He saw how heartbroken I was. He tried to get her to see how damaged I was because of her. But she wouldn't listen to him either. We left and he told me that I would never have to worry about her again. He told me that she didn't deserve to be my mother. And he told me that he had a plan. Literally the next day we got a call and she was dead. They said that she'd fallen asleep with a cigarette in her hand and caught the house on fire. But I knew in the back of my mind that Polo had something to do with it. I never said a word about it and neither did he. But I knew that he had taken care of the problem for me, yet again. The day at the funeral, my mind seemed to be set free. I seemed to instantly get better. I stopped taking my pills and everything. I didn't need them anymore. Well for a while I didn't. I didn't need them again until all of the financial stuff with my business started going on and I started to feel like I was tripping out. I started stressing. So, I had to go back on my medication. That's what happened to the sex by the way. Taking the pills seemed to affect my sex. When I don't take them, sex is fine. In case you haven't noticed that lately. The pills that Polo got me were supposed to help me balance it all out but they seemed to be messing up other things."

"Pills what pills?"

"Don't worry about that Vanessa."

"I'm Sassi!" I screamed in frustration and terror.

"I know. But you're just like Vanessa. So, as of now, you are Vanessa and you have to die."

Eddie stood up.

"Please Eddie. Please. I love you. I love you not Polo. I swear. I just want you. I just want us."

"Liar! You don't want me. No one ever wants me!"

"I do. I swear I do. I want just you."

"You're trying to trick me Vanessa."

"Eddie I'm Sassi. Your wife. The mother of your kids. You promised you would never hurt me. I'm not Vanessa. I'm not her."

"You might as well be her. You're going to die today Vanessa."

I started to wail loudly!

I am not Vanessa damn it!

"Eddie I'm not Vanessa baby. I'm not her. Wait, was Vanessa really Micki's sister?"

"What? No."

Damn!

What hadn't Micki lied about?

And why would she lie in the first place?

How did she play into all of this?

And if Vanessa wasn't really her sister then how did she know about her?

"Please Eddie. Please," I started to cry as he pointed the knife at me.

"It's too late. But don't worry. I'm going to die with you. I can't live without you. I won't let him have you. No, not you. Polo will not have you. I got to you first. You married me, not him. And I won't let him take you from me. Killing you and then killing myself is the only way."

"Eddie, who will take care of the kids?"

"They will be fine. My parents will be good to them, just like they were to me Vanessa."

"Eddie I'm Sassi. Baby, I'm Sassi."

"Okay Vanessa."

I whined and looked at my ringing phone. I could see that it was Mama again. I wished I'd answered her call or that I could tell her that I was in trouble and I needed her help.

Eddie's phone started to ring too but he didn't answer it.

"Well, let's get this over with shall we?"

He cut one of his wrists with the knife without hesitating.

"Eddie no!" I screamed as he grunted in pain.

He grabbed my hands.

They were both still in handcuffs, but he attempted to move them so that he can cut one of my wrists too.

"No!"

I started to kick at him and I squirmed all over the place.

I kicked him and moved but he finally put his weight on top of me and slit my left wrist.

"Owww!" I screamed.

Eddie just stood there as I cried and watched the blood ooze out of my wrist.

"Please Eddie. Please."

"All you had to do was love me. That's all you had to do. I love you so much."

"I love you too and I do love you. I promise you, I do Eddie. Please."

"It's too late," Eddie said about to slit his other wrist.

"Were going to sit here and die together," Eddie said but just as he finished his sentence, there was beating on the front door.

Eddie ignored it, and his ringing phone and headed to cut his wrist.

"Help!" I screamed at the top of my lungs.

Boom!

Boom!

After another bang or two, the front door flew open.

Eddie didn't move from over me but I could see that it was Polo.

Oh thank goodness.

"No Eddie! Stop. Not this time bro," Polo said.

"She doesn't love me anymore Polo. She loves you. They always love you."

"No Eddie. She loves you. I swear. She told me that today."

"You're lying for her Polo! Don't lie to me!"

Eddie was screaming. I'd never seen him act this way.

I cried underneath him and tried to get him off of me but he didn't budge.

"I'm not lying to you. I swear," Polo said and tried to walk closer but Eddie held the knife up as though he was going to stab me.

"Don't come near me Polo or I'll stab her. You know I'll do it!"

"Okay Eddie. Do you need a pill? Where are they? Let me get them. Let me help you like always."

Eddie shook his head.

"No more pills. No more pills. I'm tired of feeling this way. Everyone hurts me. People always hurt me. Even you."

"I didn't mean to. We had this talk already didn't we? I let my feelings get the best of me but it didn't happen anymore I promise. I let you have her. To let you win. You won her Eddie. She loves you. Believe me. She loves you. Trust me brother. Trust me."

Polo seemed to keep his eyes on the knife as well as both of our wrists that were dripping in blood.

"Put the knife down Eddie. Come on," Polo said.

I could feel Eddie's body relax on top of me and he acted as though he was going to get up but suddenly he shook his head.

"No. No. Not this time. You can't have her!"

Eddie screamed, put the knife high in the air and just as he started to bring the knife down on me, I heard the gun shot.

I started to scream once I saw it was Mama holding the gun.

Eddie slowly fell to the floor and I hurried to my knees beside of him.

"No Eddie! Stay with me baby. Look at me. Call 9-1-1! Now! Please!"

Mama stood there and I saw Polo fall to his knees.

"Call 9-1-1!" I screamed as Eddie's eyes started to flutter.

Mama moved but she didn't walk towards me or a phone. Instead she shut the front door.

"I-I-I love you Sassi," Eddie mumbled.

He called me Sassi! He called me Sassi and not Vanessa!

"I love you too baby. Help is on the way," I struggled to grab my phone with the handcuffs on and Mama hurried to me and took it out of my hand.

"Give me my phone Mama! Call the police! Hurry!"

Polo was still on his knees. His head was hung low.

"Eddie. Eddie. Open your eyes baby."

"I just wanted you to love me."

"And I do. I promise you I do. Come one baby. Call the fucking police now! Now! Now!" I was crying and screaming at the same time, but still Mama nor Polo moved.

Eddie coughed and blood came out of his mouth.

"Goodbye Sassi," he mumbled and with those last words, he took one last breath.

And that was it.

Eddie was gone.

"No!" I started to scream at the top of my lungs.

I cried hysterically, but Polo was even louder than I was.

He started to cry. And I do mean, cry.

He cried so hard that it shook my soul and almost made me focus more on him than on myself.

"Why! Why didn't you call for help? Why!"

I cried. I screamed at Mama but she didn't say anything.

"I could've saved him. I could've saved him. He would have listened to me," Polo mumbled through his tears.

"No he wouldn't have. And you know it. That's why you called me Polo. That's why you called me and told me to come and to be prepared," Mama said.

I laid my head on Eddie's chest.

He was gone. He was really gone.

"You killed him Mama."

"I had to. I had to shoot him to save you," she said.

Mama placed the gun on the table and stuck her hands in Eddie's pocket.

She found the keys to the handcuffs, took them off, disappeared for a second and came back with a scarf to tie tightly around my bleeding wrist.

Polo was sitting now, up against the door.

He was still crying but he was very, very still.

"How did you know? How did you know to come here? How did you know what he was going to do?"

Polo nodded towards the fireplace.

I looked at it.

After a moment or two, he stood up and went to grab one of the crystal vases. He stuck his hand in it and at the bottom there was a little camera.

Thank goodness for his stalking ass!

"One day while you and Eddie were out, I came in and placed a few over the house. I'd gotten a print of Eddie's key why he was over one day from his keys, and took it to have a copy made. I happened to log on, just to watch you, like I do sometimes, and I saw Eddie with the knife. I rushed over here as fast as I could. I thought that I wasn't going to make it in time. Like last time. Then I got here and I forgot that the key was hidden in my dashboard, but I didn't have any time to waste. I was just trying to get in to stop him. I'd called your mother on the way just in case I couldn't. I wasn't sure but I was going to try. I was going to try to stop him because had I had to choose..."

"You wouldn't have chosen me," I finished his sentence.

There was no doubt in my mind that Polo would have let Eddie kill me and cleaned up the mess.

"Actually, I think I would have."

Mama was quiet. She just seemed to be watching me.

"What was wrong with him? And why didn't anyone tell me? Why didn't I know that something was wrong with my own husband?" I questioned Polo.

He looked at Mama. She still looked at me.

"No one had to tell you what you already knew Sassi," he said.

"Where did you meet Eddie?" Polo asked me.

"At the bar with you."

"No. Where did you meet Eddie, Sassi?"

I just told him! I tried to think.

Mama opened her mouth to speak.

"Where did you meet Patrice?"

Where did I meet Patrice? I'd known her for over twenty years. I started to think.

Where did I meet Patrice?

Something came back to my memory and I gasped.

"At the hospital."

"Where did you meet Eddie? Where did you see Eddie for the first time?"

I closed my eyes and tears started to fall from my eyes.

"At the hospital."

"The first time you went you were twelve. That's where you first met Patrice. That's where you also first met Eddie."

"And me," Polo said.

I was so confused. I'd thought it was the night at the bar but some other visions started to pop in my head.

"Do you know what dementia is Sassi?"

"What? The thing that old people have? That makes them forget?"

"Not only old people have it. It's more common in elderly people but there are cases where children have it too. Maybe not as advanced, but they still do."

"So I have dementia? Memory loss?"

"Amongst other things. It got worse after the incident. We actually didn't know that you had it until the incident. I'd never paid attention to it being an issue that sometimes you couldn't remember things. And it was backwards because certain things, you could remember; like school things in such. But like memories, even from the day before or even minutes, sometimes, you just couldn't remember them. The doctors only classified it as dementia because they couldn't classify it as much else. But your memory really got shaky after the incident. You didn't really remember much before then and you only remembered what you wanted to remember after that."

"What incident?"

"When you were twelve, you saw your brother get kidnapped remember?"

"What?"

"Think Sassi."

I closed my eyes again.

"Your brother was picked up while you were outside playing one day. Remember? You were outside with him, while I'd gone into the house to answer the phone."

I was trying to remember.

"I came back outside and he was gone. I asked you where he was but you'd said that you didn't know. You were right there, yet you couldn't remember the car or the person that snatched him. You couldn't remember anything. We found him three days later. In the woods. Dead."

What? My brother was dead?

What the hell was she talking about?

Maybe I'd had another brother that I'd forgotten about.

"You blamed yourself. You were never the same after that. None of us were. That's when your father turned into an alcoholic remember?"

I shook my head. I was still stuck on the other part.

"I don't understand."

"You had to be sent to the hospital for a little while after that. You started acting weird. You were so bothered. You blamed yourself for your brother's death. At first you acted depressed. And then you just started acting out. So we tried to get you some help."

"Wait. What are you talking about Mama? So there's something else wrong with me? Other than memory loss?"

"Those doctors didn't know what they were talking about. They started trying to say all kinds of stuff about you, and even had me send you to a hospital to try to figure it out. That's where you met Patrice. Patrice was having problems dealing with her mother's death. But really I think that she was just acting out. She had decent sense to me. Her father was just ashamed of her and kept sticking her in there every chance that he could. That's where you met her. Even after a while, whenever she would have to go back you started saying that she was at camp, or cheerleading or something. But she was always at the hospital. But I always wanted you home. You only had to go there twice and after the second time, I said never again. I love you. And whatever was going on with you, I just thought that love would cure you."

I just couldn't put it all together.

"The doctors thought you were acting out on depression and guilt and things like that. You stayed there for a little while, but you seemed to improve. Then you had a few episodes and I sent you back; it was one time in your teens, and you came back with Micki."

Huh?

"How? I met Micki through Patrice."

"No baby. You met Micki in your mind. She's made up. She doesn't really exist. We all just pretend with you as if she does."

What the fuck!

"No. You're lying!"

"No. I'm not. Call her then."

I grabbed my phone.

"I can't call her that number is disconnected. When she moved she cut off the number."

Mama looked at Polo.

"He disconnected that line that he would use to pretend sometimes. She found it online and got suspicious," Polo spoke up.

What?

"Oh,. Yeah, you are so nosey. It's like your mind always makes you believe you are some kind of private eye detective, or investigator or something. You have always, always thought that you could figure out any and everything," Mama said.

What the hell was going on?

"Micki is all in your mind Sassi. Every conversation with her is in your head. Or a hallucination. Or even in your dreams. Sometimes you confuse them as reality. One doctor tried to classify you as schizophrenia, but I told him to shove it. You are just acting out because of the guilt from the incident. But yes, sometimes you get confused with what's real."

"Which is why we made you think that you were dreaming about Vanessa," Polo spoke up again. "We knew either you wouldn't remember or you wouldn't be able to separate a dream from reality. But you did."

Mama looked at Polo as though she hadn't approved of that part but she didn't say anything.

Micki was all in my head?

Like an imaginary friend?

Huh?

"Look, okay, look."

Mama stuck her hand in a purse that I hadn't even noticed that she had been carrying. She must have carried it to place the gun in it.

She handed me a piece of paper.

"It's a copy of Patrice's will. Seeing is believing."

I looked at it. I was the only one listed as a beneficiary.

Micki's name was nowhere to be found.

"This doesn't make sense."

"You've had this imaginary Micki for years. Everyone is aware of her. Even Patrice had issues but she knew that Micki wasn't real. But we all loved you, so we made you comfortable. We've all just went along with it all this time."

"I almost messed up at the grocery store. When you said that Micki was Vanessa's sister. Your statement caught me off guard. Had you been paying attention, you would have caught on to it. Think Sassi," Polo said.

"Sassi, your brother was killed and Micki doesn't exist."

"But Micki was the one who told Eddie that I was having an affair, and she told me that Eddie had fooled around with Patrice."

"No. She didn't. Eddie found out that you and Polo were creeping around on his own. And you remembered a conversation that you overheard from years ago between Eddie and Patrice. You forgot about it. You told me what you heard , the day before your wedding, but when I asked you about it on your wedding day, you had no idea what I was talking about. So

I left it alone. Micki didn't tell you anything. Your memory told you. You remember pieces of things but sometimes you remember them in a different way. You make up something or a story behind it. In that situation, you made it as though Micki told you. I'll admit, sometimes we all use Micki to our benefit. To get you to understand something or even to hide something else. But she doesn't exist, Sassi. Micki isn't real."

This was crazy! And apparently I was crazy too!

"Micki isn't real."

"No. She's not baby," Mama said.

"But I saw you with her Polo. On one of your video tapes."

"No. You saw me with someone else and you saw what you wanted to see."

"You hallucinate sometimes Sassi, that's all it is baby. But whatever you remember, think, or anything concerning Micki is not real. It is all in your head. It is what you make yourself see. Micki is imaginary. Your imaginary friend. Nothing more."

"But Patrice is real? Well, she was. She was my real friend."

"Yes."

"What about the cops? And everything?"

"That was real."

"So she really didn't die from a tumor? Someone really did kill her right?"

"Yes."

"Who?"

Mama took a deep breath.

"You."

What did she just say? Did she just say me?

"You killed her Sassi. The fact that you remembered and hearing her confess to the Eddie situation as well as all of the stuff with your father, I assume it made you snap or something."

"How? No. I didn't kill her."

"Yes you did Sassi," Polo said.

"I was watching you. I followed you late one night to Patrice's. I'm not sure how you knew she was back in town but she was. Maybe you were just going over to mess up her house or something, no one knows, but you went into the house late in the middle of the night. When you came out, you left the front door wide open so I knew something was wrong. You drove away. And I went in behind you. Patrice was in bed with a pillow on her face. The medicine bottles beside her bed told me that she was probably good and drugged up on some of her meds, and you simply over powered her. If she tried to fight you back, she was probably so doped up that she was destined to lose that battle. You killed her. I called your mother, and I went to work making it look like she had a tumor. I did all of the paperwork, fake labels, medicine switch outs and everything while your mother got rid of anything you might have touched. That's why she had Patrice's necklace. You seemed to have ripped it off and threw it on the floor. Or maybe there was some kind of struggle between you two. No one will ever know. Unless you remember it."

"No. I didn't kill her. No. I didn't kill my best friend."

"Yes baby. You did. I was the one that acted as though I'd come to visit her and found her dead. Though I already knew she was, I played the part. I told the officers that I was like a mother figure to her because she was my daughter's best friend and had lost her mother years ago. It wasn't hard for them to believe it and of course her father cosigned on your friendship. I'm the one that "found" her and reported her dead."

I shook my head and tried to understand.

"I told them that she'd told me that she was sick prior to, but that I hadn't known what was wrong with her. The findings of the tumor stuff made the statement look more believable and not to mention that she really had changed her will only two days before. It made it look like she was really expecting to die sometime soon. But I think that she really did change it out of guilt, and because that was the day that I'd talked to her."

Poor Patrice.

"Maybe she felt guilty for all she'd done to both of us and decided to go up there and leave you all of that money, because now that we are being honest, I cussed her out from her to Mexico. I called her everything but a child of the most high God. I told her that she was a whore and that not only had she ruined my marriage but she'd also contributed to ruining yours. I knew I shouldn't have said all of that to her because she had problems too, but I couldn't help myself. And I hadn't even known the other stuff that you told me. I could have only imagined what I would have said then. So, maybe that's why she changed her will. Or maybe she changed it because she was leaving town again, and for good that time, for real. I'd found print-outs of houses for her to buy in another country. I think that she had just come back to tie up loose ends. Either way, it just made the tumor story look a lot better. How did you know that she was even back in town Sassi?"

I shook my head.

"I don't know. I don't know. So, Micki didn't go with me to the lawyer's office? She isn't the one that told me that Patrice had died?"

"Micki is only in your head Sassi. The lawyer was the one that told you that Patrice died from a tumor. I was standing in the back of the room the entire time. Watching you act as though Micki was there with you the whole time but she wasn't. I was the one that told you to meet me there. When you got there, I tried to speak to you but you were having a whole conversation with yourself, with Micki, so I just followed you in. He was the one that had to break the news. He knew all about "Micki" because I told him. I've been seeing him for a while, Sassi. He is the man that I was married to before your father. He was my first husband. The man that I left to be with your dad. He forgave me and we've been trying to work things out for a while now. But because he cares for me, he went along with it. He didn't have to, but for me he did. He even made up some little letter to Micki too as though it was in the will to make you feel better. But there was nothing there for Micki because she is only in your head."

"So this isn't a joke? I'm really crazy?"

"No. I don't like to call it that. You have spells. You have an imagination. And a little memory loss. All of those years, you were harmless. It was simply the dreams, acting out here there, Micki, and other hallucinations for a long time. We didn't know that you would kill until…"

"Until what?"

"Until you hit the woman, Katrina, that approached you in the store about us and the sex tapes," Polo said.

"What?"

"That story I told you? The one about Micki hitting her and leaving the scene? It was you. It was you Sassi."

No. Hell no.

"Think."

I was trying.

"Bad news or something that makes you angry triggers it apparently. Whatever "it" is, we don't know, but here lately it hasn't been a good thing. The doctors wanted you institutionalized but me and Eddie promised to take care of you. He's been sneaking medicine into your food and drink for years. Especially in those smoothies that he would make for you most mornings. That's why I wanted you to stay in your marriage and around Eddie. And when he couldn't, sometimes I would find a way to get them in you. Even Patrice would do it when Eddie would inform her that he needed to get some medicine in you. Whether we had to crunch the pills up or whatever, we all got them in you. And there would be sometimes that you would remember that you had some issues, and take them yourself. It just depends."

Polo nodded.

"I wasn't following her Sassi. I was following you. You followed her from the café after you got off of the phone with me. I was right outside. I watched you trial her and so I trialed you. She pulled up at home, and you sat there for hours and I sat right there with you. I wondered what you were doing. I thought maybe you thought that I was going to come over her house or something, and maybe you planned on confronting me or something. I wasn't sure."

I braced myself for what he was about to say next.

"When she came back out, a little while later, as it was getting dark you followed her. She turned down a small side street and it was like you instincts told you to take the opportunity, and you slammed your car into hers. You got out of your car to look at her. I don't think that you meant to kill her. You even laughed aloud and then when you opened the door and saw that she was probably dead, you screamed. You got back into your car and then you drove off. I called Eddie. He confirmed when you got there that your car was wrecked. Your forehead was even bleeding but somehow you acting like nothing was wrong. He said you came straight into the house, knot on your head and all and sat at your laptop. Do you remember that night?"

I think I did. But I didn't remember the accident.

"He told you to write for the rest of the night and we handled everything else. We went to work with covering everything up. I done everything that I told you that I did for Micki, except it was for you. I wiped the scene, picked up parts from your car. Eddie drove your car to a friend to have it crushed, and then I purchased you a brand new one, same year, make and color, the next morning, and had it sitting outside waiting for you before you woke up. We fixed it. Being rich has its perks and when everyone thought that I was wasting money, I was making connections. Plenty of them. With you and Eddie, I just never knew what I might need one day. Once you killed Patrice, I went back and stuck a few tiny things, here and there, at the scene that would have pointed towards her if the police ever really went looking, since Patrice was already dead. But they never did."

I looked at Eddie's body.

We were really just sitting there talking as though he wasn't laying there dead. Why couldn't he have told me everything that I was hearing now? Why hadn't he been honest with me?

"What was wrong with Eddie?"

"His mama, his real one messed him up years ago. Nothing more than anxiety and depression. And some acceptance issues.

But that was pretty much it. He only had to go to the hospital because he was ordered to, when he "accidentally" killed Vanessa. He got off but considering that the judge could see the history of things that he'd been through, and medicines that he'd been prescribed, he thought that it would be beneficial for him to spend some time there, just to make sure that he didn't flip out from depression or guilt or something. That's where I actually saw you for the first time. You were laughing and joking around. I was visiting Eddie and we sat at the same table as you and Patrice. You were visiting Patrice. You weren't admitted at the time, and you seemed normal until you were about to leave and you told "Micki" to come on, but no one was right there. I remember thinking, she might need to stay here for a little while herself, not knowing your issues."

"Sometimes Patrice's trips, weren't always trips. Sometimes she was going away for issues. To get her mind back on track. But she figured out the more she traveled and saw the world, she felt better. She felt alive. It was being home that always brought back painful memories for her. That's why she was always going away."

"So DJ, my brother is dead?"

"Has been for years."

"Who car did I drive to Polo's that day then?"

"Your father's. You had a spare key. I hadn't driven it in years. I came home and it was gone. Later on that night, you brought it back, got into your car, and drove home."

"So he didn't have a baby with Micki?"

"Micki doesn't exist Sassi. Anything you have ever said about or in reference to Micki, anything you remember with Micki, you made it up. All of it. I don't have any grandkids, but yours."

"And everyone knew?"

"Yes. Everyone is aware of your problems. Even Eddie's parents knew. They understood because of his issues."

"And I met him in the hospital?"

"Initially. The next time I saw you, was at the gas station with Patrice. The time I told you about. The night at the bar was actually the third time. I was there with Eddie. You were there with Patrice. Just Patrice."

I tried to remember.

"And you wanted me knowing that I was crazy?"

"You were still beautiful to me. I didn't see you as crazy. Hell, I didn't see Eddie as crazy. He had a good heart. Life just hadn't always been fair to him. But Eddie made his move on you. I guess he wanted to finally get the girl. He wanted to get the girl of my dreams since he could never seem to get his. And he did."

I remembered him telling me that.

I looked at my dead husband still on the floor.

I couldn't see the blood underneath him, but I knew that it was going to leave a terrible stain from him being there for so long.

Oh Eddie.

"We were trying to keep all of this from you. But you saw the tape and of course Eddie told me. That night, he'd asked me to come by. When I got there, that's when he told me that you knew about Vanessa. He didn't know that he'd had it wrong until afterwards. Once I watched the tape, I knew that you were talking about what you heard him say in regards to his real mother. Not Vanessa. But that wasn't until after."

"And Micki never came there that day? The day you caused me to pass out?"

"Micki isn't real Sassi," Mama answered as though she was trying to beat it into my head.

"It was just me."

That was why her number wasn't in my call log…right?

I'd thought that they'd erased it.

But I'd never been on the phone with her; at least not for real anyway. And anytime I thought I did, they had another line pretending? This was crazy!

"I made you pass out, got you to swallow the pill, covered up you taking the pregnancy test and we tried to make it look like Eddie had never said Vanessa's name. You remembered little parts because you woke up Sassi. But you would blame it on Micki as if she told you. But it was your memory trying to tell you instead. It was almost as though Micki was just another form of who you wanted to be. She was the outspoken, loud, ride or die personality that we assume that maybe you wish that you were or would like to be. But we tried to cover it all up. I guess he was just nervous about you finding out the truth about him. He knew all of your truths. But he didn't want you to know his."

Damn you Eddie!

I couldn't help but wonder if he'd really even been giving me my medicine since he obviously hadn't been taking his.

"And this is real?"

"Yes. Why do you think I was always watching? I was watching Eddie. I was watching you. I've always felt like I've owed Eddie my life. Literally. He cared about me just as much as I cared about him. So I always wanted to make sure that mentally, he was okay. He knew that I would do anything for him. That's why he'd thought I killed his real mother. But I didn't."

"You didn't?"

"No. I went by there but when I got there, the house was already on fire. I was going to tell her about Eddie's mental state and beg her to understand that he needed her, but the house was in flames. I'm the one that made the 9-1-1 call. But the next day, when I went to see if Eddie had heard the news, he was better than ever. He was like, normal. Like her death had set him free. So, I let him be free. I still made sure he took his medicine, but since then, he had been fine. Until stress of his business started to get to him and especially after what we did to him."

"You knew better," Mama said. "We all knew how unstable you and Eddie were. Polo knew not to cross that line, which is why I was so nasty about it and tried to stop it before it got out of hand. I didn't want any unnecessary mess or problems. I didn't want things to get out of hand. But they did."

"I'm sorry. I fought it for years. My feelings got the best of me. That day that he showed up with that gun, he really would have killed us both Sassi. He really would have."

Polo was a fool!

Why would he even cross that line with me knowing Eddie's history? And knowing my truth?

"I held my feelings back for years because I knew they were nothing but trouble. And that's all that we have caused. Trouble."

This was so much to take in.

I got off of the floor and sat on the couch.

"Once you met Eddie and especially once your first child, you were doing a lot better. But Eddie would catch you talking to Micki often but other than that, you were pretty okay. So we just let you be."

"But I went to Micki's wedding. I was there."

"It was all in your mind Sassi. Sometimes you dream these things and other times you are wide awake and really acting them out as if it is actually happening and as if Micki is actually there with you. You would say that you guys were taking the kids to the park. You would have conversations with us about her or say that she said this. And we would just go along with it. It was better than constantly telling you that something was wrong with you. We'd been telling you that for years. That only seemed to make things worse. So we stopped and just went along. Like now. I've been telling you that Micki isn't real, but you continue insisting that your memories of her actually happened. So we just stopped telling you. As long as you weren't hurting yourself or anybody else, we just let you live. But then you did hurt somebody Sassi. Patrice was one of them."

The more I thought about what they were saying to me, the more I started to remember some of the things.

I was overwhelmed. I was scared.

"So now what? I go back to the hospital? Eddie is dead. Now what am I supposed to do?"

I started to cry.

"I'll take care of you," Polo spoke up.

Mama and I both looked at him.

"Polo I'm crazy. I'm a murderer. I see imaginary people. I belong in a hospital."

"No. You belong with me. I'll take care of you. Until my dying day," Polo said.

He stood up and came closer.

"You would do that? Why? After this mess I've caused. Eddie and Patrice would both still be here if it wasn't for me."

"I'll take care of you. I've been watching your back for years. I've been helping make sure you were okay for years. I can and I will take care of you."

Mama was now crying too.

"Okay. Well go. I'll call the police. I'll say something and take whatever blame I have to. I'll say he attacked me or something and I shot him," Mama said.

"No Mama. I'm going to need you. I can't lose you too. Not now."

I looked at Eddie.

I wished things would have been different.

I wished that he'd never met me.

He would have probably been much better off.

"Polo."

"Yes?"

"Mama can't go to jail for this. Not like this. Not because of me. Can you take care of this? Like you did with Vanessa? And Patrice?"

Polo nodded.

"I wouldn't have it any other way," he said.

~***~

"Hey you," Polo said.

I smiled at him as I swallowed my pills.

I'd gone to the doctor and for now I was remembering to take them. I was determined to get better.

I was determined to be normal. For real this time.

Polo had somehow pulled off making things look like Eddie was involved in a break-in gone bad and had been shot in the back.

He'd kicked the door open already, so it did kind of look like a forced entry and as Mama drove away with me that night, he was doing what he did best.

Creating a cover up.

"I love you beautiful," he said.

He vowed to always keep me in the loop and be honest with me about my condition and remind me daily that I had to take my medicine and what I was dealing with so that I wouldn't try to block out the truth and forget.

"Hey."

"How are you feeling?"

"Good."

"You take your medicine?"

"Just did," I said behind him as he headed to see what the boys were doing.

We were now at his house. There was no way I was going back to the one that Eddie and I shared.

Eddie had been buried, and as far as everyone else knew, his killers were long gone.

Polo came back into the room.

My phone started to vibrate, and I answered the private call.

"Hello?"

"Did you find out who Vanessa was yet?" Micki said.

"Yes Micki I did, and…" before I could finish my sentence, Polo snatched my phone.

"Sassi. Micki isn't real. Look."

I looked at the phone and realized that it said Mama instead of Micki.

I exhaled.

"Don't worry. We've got this," Polo said and told Mama that I would call her back later.

"What if I can't do this?"

"You will do this. In time the medicine will make it better. Just don't forget me anytime soon," Polo joked.

"I could never forget you."

"Well, the kids are watching a movie. Maybe we should make one?" Polo grinned.

"Pinch me," I said to him.

He did and I smiled.

"Just making sure that this moment was real. I love you Polo."

He smiled as he kissed me.

"I love you too."

My phone started to vibrate and I wondered if it was "Micki" calling back.

Polo keep kissing me.

"It's not Micki. She isn't real," Polo repeated and started to take off my clothes.

What's a woman to do when she marries the wrong man? When the reality is, all along, she should have married his best friend?

Well, now that the wrong husband was dead...I was about to find out!

****

The End

Author B.M. Hardin's contact info:

TEXT BMBOOKS to 22828 for more release updates

Facebook: http://www.facebook.com/authorbm

Twitter: @BMHardin1

Instagram: @bm_hardin

Email:bmhardinbooks@gmail.com